Queens' Row

a novel

Hannah Huber

Introduction by Leslie Trew Magraw

Amsterdam Academy Press

Self-publishing powered by
Amsterdam Academy Press
www.amsterdamacademy.com

This book is a work of fiction. Any references to historical events, real people,
or real places are used fictitiously. Other names, characters, places, and events
are products of the author's imagination, and any resemblance to actual events or
places or persons, living or dead, is entirely coincidental.

1st edition
ISBN paperback 978-9-0903-7459-8
ISBN ebook 979-8-2230-4690-5

This book was set in a modern adaptation of a type designed by the first William
Caslon (1692-1766). The first copies of the Declaration of Independence and
the first paper currency distributed to the citizens of the newborn nation were
printed in the Caslon typeface.

Cover artwork: Joe Webb, joewebbart.com
Cover design: Glenn Doherty, glenndoherty.work & Cigdem Guven, crocusfield.com
Layout: Lisa Hall, lemonberry.com

FSC
www.fsc.org
FSC® C117418

Introduction

Everyone has heard of Gettysburg. (From my experience, most people think it's in Virginia, but that's a different story for another day.) When called to mind, Gettysburg evokes a somber deference to the past and an encapsulation of the enduring tension between feuding factions that we still see playing out today in Congress and around the dinner table.

In popular culture, Gettysburg seems to be frozen in time—it has no past before the Civil War and no identity beyond it. But Gettysburg did exist before the war and it existed after the smoke cleared in town. In fact, its story is still unfolding.

If you've ever been to Gettysburg you can attest to the fact that it's a town obsessed with Abraham Lincoln—and that's for good reason. In addition to being the unwitting site of the bloodiest single battle of the war, President Lincoln's famous address expanded the meaning of "what they did here" so that Gettysburg became an enduring symbol of the promise of democracy outlined in the Declaration of Independence.

Dwight Eisenhower felt that profundity, too. When he was at West Point, in 1915, his class of young cadets visited Gettysburg to study the battle. Then, as the nation prepared to join the fray in World War I, Ike was tapped to remain on the homefront to train the newly formed Tank Corps at Camp Colt, located on ground trod during Pickett's doomed charge. He even helped keep the citizens of Gettysburg safe when an outbreak of the Spanish Flu threatened to spread beyond the camp in 1919.

Having never put down roots as a couple—the Eisenhowers were a quintessential Army family, moving from house to house many times during Ike's burgeoning military career—Mamie pressed her husband to purchase a permanent home for their family as the now celebrated WWII general considered a presidential run. In 1950, the Eisenhowers gravitated to a place that held special meaning for them and bought a 187-acre farm overlooking the hallowed battlefield and the Blue Ridge Mountains to the west.

Ike would go on to win the presidency in two landslide elections in 1952 and 1956. All the while the First Family treated their Pennsylvania home, pains takingly renovated by Mamie, as an almost sacred rural refuge where they could escape the pressures of Washington and be themselves. It was also a place Ike brought world leaders like Charles De Gaulle and Nikita Khrushchev to put them at ease—along with the official presidential retreat, Shangri-la, which was a mere 20 miles from the farm. You may know it as Camp David; Eisenhower renamed it in honor of his father and his grandson, both named David, in 1953.

And so if Lincoln is Gettysburg's first founding father, Eisenhower is its second.

Lincoln, a famously remote figure, spent just 25 hours in Gettysburg, but left a lasting mark on its destiny with his words. Eisenhower, on the other hand, was a man of the people. He lived, worked, and golfed among the town's ordinary denizens. He raised Angus cattle, he played bridge and hosted barbecues, he worshiped with his family at the local Presbyterian Church. His legacy is far more mundane and far more human.

Eisenhower left his mark on the town, too, and the town found ways to honor him; a local school, hotel, and leadership institute are all named for the 34th president. And the First Family's farm—the deed to which was personally transferred by Ike and Mamie, with an eye to their legacy, to the federal government in 1967—has been open to the public as a national historic site since 1980.

But during the Eisenhower Era in Gettysburg, from 1950 until his death in 1969—almost two whole decades—the family provided their adopted home town with a kind of excitement and glamor Gettysburg has never seen before or since. This is just what my dear friend, Hannah Huber, brings to life in such vivid relief in her new novel, *Queens' Row*.

Against the soundtrack of the Everly Brothers and with the threat of World War III on the doorstep, Huber weaves a tale about Professor Grace Gilmartin and her friends who occupy the coveted lounge chairs on "Queens' Row" at Gettysburg Country Club. Women were on the cusp of a revolution, but in 1960 there were mere stirrings of what was to come.

Her story incorporates elements from her own life, her mother's life, and from the life and time of her father's mother, her beloved Grandma Betty, to whom this book is dedicated. The throughline for each of these generations was and is the Gettysburg Country Club, which, quite sadly, closed in 2008.

When I think about my childhood—I grew up with Hannah and we spent countless hours making forts out of lounge chairs and jumping off the high dive—the country club calls to mind the smell of Hawaiian Tropic tanning oil, face-reddening crushes on lifeguards, frozen Snickers bars and piled-high Club sandwiches, and the monotonous repetition of "Marco, Polo."

It was a special place for all of us, and each generation had its own version of "Queens' Row"—the popular, pretty moms who sat in a line facing the pool and seemed to spend all of their time comparing notes on their children, spreading the latest gossip, and perfecting their tans. Grace fits in with these women—and she doesn't.

As someone who doesn't have children myself, I can strongly relate to the ambivalence Grace feels about "motherhood." Compulsory motherhood is a deeply embedded cultural norm in our society—and one that few talk about or even notice unless they are experiencing fertility challenges.

Weighing whether to have children can be especially difficult for women approaching middle age, as they have established an identity and career and lifestyle outside the strictures of motherhood that they are loath to give up. Yet if they remain childless, either by intention or due to the mitigating factors of age and circumstance, they stand to be out of step with their peers, accused of being selfish and out of touch, and confront lingering regrets that they "missed their window."

This is why *Queens' Row* is at once deeply personal and universal. Women of all generations can recognize their own struggles within the pages of this book. The "damned if you do, damned if you don't"-edness of prioritizing career advancement or forgoing familial obligations to pursue one's dreams. When these things are present in a man's life they are accepted as par for the course, or even viewed as badges of honor. When women pursue these avenues, they can expect to face judgment, criticism, or rejection, even in 2023.

Living in today's world we see that the Equal Rights Amendment, first introduced a century ago, in 1923, is still languishing in Congress, that Roe was overturned, further eroding our reproductive rights, that women are paid a fraction of what their male counterparts earn, and that, despite the expectation that all women become mothers, we receive little support once we do.

Queens' Row lets us see how far women have come, but also how far we still have to go in order to be ourselves without the world weighing in.

Leslie Trew Magraw

Betty Huber (standing on the right) with her friends prior to a dinner at the White House, May 2, 1960

For Elizabeth Gleason Huber (Grandma Betty).
Thank you for your love and storytelling. You were
and remain an unstoppable force.

1
GCC

Saturday, June 18, 1960

Professor Grace Gilmartin sat where she always sat, near the table with the yellow pom pom-fringed parasol, just behind the lifeguard stand. The third lounge chair in made her feel more comfortable, less exposed. By positioning herself there, she was also setting herself up to be within optimal earshot of town gossip. Guests of the Gettysburg Country Club had to pass her to enter the pool, but because she wasn't in the end chair, people would continue to talk, not realizing she was listening to their uncensored stories, all along. This is how she was the first to know that Ethel had failed her diet, again, Jack had a snoring problem, and lifeguard Mary had a crush on Bobby. The GCC—that's what members called it—made her feel like a local; she didn't even have to present a pass when entering. She simply showed up, smiled, waved, and put orders from the snack bar on her tab. Grace liked to be the first to arrive, as soon as the country club opened—11:00 a.m. By the time she started unpacking her pool bag, Mary, who also happened to be Grace's teaching assistant that semester, was already testing the chlorine levels in the pool.

"It's going to be a hot one today, Professor Gilmartin."

"That's what I heard. Eighty-eight degrees is high for mid-June, don't you think?" Grace began applying baby oil to her slender arms and legs, taking care to avoid getting it on her one-piece seersucker swimsuit.

"It sure is."

Mary went about her opening rituals, lining up the chairs, wiping down tables, and grabbing herself a cold Coca-Cola before climbing up into the stand. She switched on her radio and turned it down to a soft volume. Grace could hear 'Cathy's Clown' by the Everly Brothers. Although she liked the song, she was starting to get sick of it—it was all the radio ever played these days. Not to mention she had heard it that night at the White House, last month. A night she wished had never happened. Or was that even true?

The song ended and an errant drop of baby oil landed on the concrete. Once every exposed inch of her body was covered in oil, she smoothed out her blue and white striped towel, carefully sat down, and put on her sunglasses. She glanced over at the clock hanging on the clubhouse—11:10. The other girls should be rolling in soon. Maybe Grace could fit in a few laps first. Lois, her best girlfriend, was coming straight from the golf course. Her grandfather had taught her how to play and, even though it was never explicitly mentioned, it seemed to be an unspoken rule that only women who played well were "allowed" out on the course. Grace admired how driven Lois was; she seemed to master everything she did, whether it be golf, or editing articles for the local newspaper. Jane, on the other hand, was always late, no matter the occasion. Grace suspected she secretly enjoyed building suspense for her arrival, but her vivacious laugh made up for it. Olga—who was an import, like Grace, having moved to town last year—would show up occasionally. She was the quietest of the bunch, and kept herself busy as owner-operator of the local dry cleaners. Olga and Grace's shared outsider status meant they had to make more of an effort to fit in, which was difficult seeing as they were both introverts.

Grace stared at the clear blue water. She'd never felt so alone in her life as she had these past five weeks. Who was she to tell? Her current state was so fragile, yet also powerful enough to change her life, multiple lives, forever. She crossed her arms over her lower abdomen reflexively. The sun's rays bounced off the pool's placid surface, creating a dazzling prismatic pattern that left Grace mesmerized, completely lost in thought. She decided to go for a quick swim.

Grace adjusted the strap of her goggles, making sure they fit snugly around her head. She tucked her hair into her daisy-embossed swim cap and lowered her shoulders into the water, allowing her body to adjust to the cool temperature. She watched her hands glide in front of her, pushing the water away like cobwebs. The water was refreshing and for a moment she felt peaceful and weightless, focusing only on her breath. Her mother had taught her how to swim, how to continue kicking while keeping her arm movements going in a steady rhythm. Grace looked down at the thick black stripe on the bottom of the pool that marked her lane.

The longer she swam, the more scattered her thoughts became. She could feel her heart pounding as she thought of her husband, Ed, and how she had lied to him about something so momentous. She hated lying. Now she carried not one, but two powerful secrets. It was suffocating. Ed, who had been nothing but kind to her during their eleven years of marriage, didn't deserve this. But it wasn't like she meant for any of this to happen. She thought about how things might have been if she had made different choices. If her mother had made a different choice. Her life felt like one big trial and error, hit or miss. She was always making do with the cards life dealt her, all the while feeling alone and scared. Did fate even exist, or was everything determined by circumstance? As she swam, a sense of panic overtook her and she foundered. Bubbles of sobs erupted around her face as she slowly sank to the bottom. After a few seconds, Grace pushed off with her feet and grabbed for the edge of the pool. Mary saw something was wrong and ran over to her. She knelt down and placed her hand on Grace's shoulder. "Professor Gilmartin! Are you okay?"

Grace, panting, took a moment to catch her breath. She removed her goggles, which were all fogged up.

"Yes. Yes, I'm fine. Not to worry. I suppose I'm not in as good shape as I thought I was."

"Can I get you anything? Water?" Mary asked, concerned.

"No. No, I'm fine. Thank you, Mary."

Grace climbed out of the pool and lay down on her lounge chair. She watched her chest rise and fall as her breath stabilized. As she turned her head toward the fence, she could have sworn she saw her mother standing there with calm, apologetic eyes, her arms outstretched. Impossible. Her eyes were playing tricks on her. She had not seen her mother in twenty-five years.

"Good morning, dear!" Lois said in her sing-song voice. "Wakey, wakey. You're daydreaming." Lois plopped down on the chair beside Grace and started taking off her golf cleats. She wiped the sweat dripping from her forehead with a small towel.

Grace, startled, sat up straight to make her torso seem flatter. "How did you play?" She glanced toward the fence, but her mother was gone.

"We only played nine holes. It's way too hot. I'm going to change quickly in the locker room. Do you want anything while I'm down there? Maybe a Coke or something?" Before Grace had a chance to answer, Jane came waltzing in across the hot pavement, her sheer red cover up blowing in the breeze.

"Yoo-hoo, morning ladies!" Jane called as she slid off her gold sandals. "You headed down to the snack bar? I'll take whatever Grace is having. Just put it on my tab—2885."

"Gee, aren't you feeling generous today?" Lois said, picking up her bag. "Is there a reason for this sudden goodwill?" Jane was notorious for never having money—or credit.

"Well, I was going to save this news for later, but since you asked...Dale just gave me a raise! You're looking at the highest paid waitress in Gettysburg! Well, at Faber's at least."

Faber's was the place everyone went in search of good conversation, a fountain soda, or simply a good excuse to get out of the house. Located on the town square, next to the Hotel Gettysburg, entering Faber's was like entering a familiar dream. Red leather swivel chairs lined the shiny stainless steel rimmed counter, and cozy wooden booths graced the walls. One could argue that most of the men in Gettysburg went to Faber's to see Jane Kendall—although no one would ever admit that. Everybody loved Jane; she could do things most women couldn't, like whistle through her teeth and play baseball. With her heart-shaped mouth, golden hair that sparkled in the sun, and a figure that stayed the same no matter how many milkshakes she drank, Jane was as local as could be—third-generation Gettysburgian, born and raised. She had even been crowned Gettysburg High School's Prom Queen. Men never messed with Jane, mostly because if they did they would have to deal with her combative husband, Jack. But they sure loved her coming around to refill their coffee. Jane always believed that she was destined for better things. Her dream was to be a Hollywood star. At least working at Faber's gave her some sense of independence—and a stage, albeit of a different kind.

Lois clapped her hands. "That's wonderful news, Jane! Well, in that case, I'll definitely let you treat today. I'll be right back."

Before Lois had a chance to leave for the locker room, Olga arrived, wearing a black one-piece bathing suit and large dark sunglasses, her jet black hair pulled back into a tight ponytail.

"Just in time; want anything from the snack bar?" Lois touched Olga's arm, as she headed toward the steps.

"I'll have a Coke, please." Olga laid out her towel on one of the free lounge chairs. "Is Barbara coming today?"

"I'm not sure, but sit wherever. We can always grab another chair," Jane said. "Hey, did you get an invite to Ethel's next week? She's hosting bridge club this month."

"Yes," Grace replied. "She asked me to bring my

deviled eggs." Grace grabbed the latest *Time* magazine from her pool bag, emblazoned with "Khrushchev Attacks the U.S.," lit a cigarette, and started reading. Minutes later, Lois came back with four bottles of Coke and cups filled to the brim with ice.

"Can you believe this crap?!" Grace asked, exasperated, as Lois handed out the cups. "Ike was diplomatic enough to say Khrushchev was a dynamic man with an arresting personality at the summit last week, and that son of a bitch called him 'spineless.' He said Ike could run a children's home, but not a nation." Grace took a long drag of her cigarette.

"Maybe he's right," Olga offered, without moving a muscle—even the plastic goggles she put over her eyes to allow for a minimal tan line had stayed in place.

Grace rolled her eyes. "What planet are you from? Khrushchev is bad news, Olga."

Since Lois worked at and co-owned the *Gettysburg Times* with her husband Robert, she kept Grace, Jane, and Olga abreast of the latest international news, and they just couldn't seem to get enough. The fact that Dwight Eisenhower had bought a sprawling farm in Gettysburg in 1950, as he had been preparing his first presidential run, only fueled their political curiosity. In the intervening years, Ike, and his wife Mamie, had been making the

80-mile drive north from Washington, spending any free moment they could in the pastoral Pennsylvania countryside. It was common knowledge around town that, when the president retired the following year the farm would become a permanent full-time home for the First Couple. As each day crept closer to the end of his term, the energy and tension in town grew.

There were two schools of thought about the Eisenhowers among the locals. Some loved that they were there and ate up the fact that they brought attention and glamour to Gettysburg, whose only other claim to fame began and ended with the Civil War. Others—those who whispered—"Our town is being overrun by the press," "They have no business here," "They should stay in Washington"—hated the notoriety and yearned for simpler times.

Lois and Jane loved the fact that the president and first lady had chosen Gettysburg to retire to. After all, they knew their town was a special place—more than just a battlefield tourist trap, thanks to Lincoln's famous speech. Olga seemed indifferent. Grace liked the Eisenhowers, but she didn't like the effect they had had on her friends. Though she didn't blame them or find it at all surprising; even Grace had to admit that it was hard to resist being star struck.

Grace's friends wanted nothing more than to be best friends with Ike's son, Lt. Col. John Eisenhower, and his wife, Barbara, who had moved with their four children to a charming old house nearby Ike and Mamie's farm in 1959. With the Blue Ridge Mountains as a backdrop, Gettysburg offered them a slice of ordinary life and was slightly cooler than muggy Washington.

Lois was the one who had instigated a connection with the Eisenhowers. When she saw Barbara come into the cleaners to get a skirt hemmed, she seized the opportunity and invited her to play bridge with her friends once a month. Lois was as proud as a peacock when she brought Barbara to the next bridge club night, escorting her to each of the tables and introducing the group to her "new friend, Barbara." She had caught a big, famous fish in a small pond; there was no way she was letting go of that line. Soon thereafter, the playdates started—Barbara's daughter, Susan, was the same age as Lois's daughter, Carol. And Barbara's oldest son, David, was the same age as Jane's oldest, Michael. Thus, the relatability, cocktail socializing, and carpooling began.

Grace would never forget when Barbara showed up at bridge night, either. Barbara wore an emerald-green satin skirt and what looked like an expensive pearl necklace. Grace, usually the smartest dressed woman in the group, felt dowdy and underdressed in her gray wool skirt and cream-colored blouse. Her brown heels felt old-fashioned next to Barbara's designer shoes that she'd casually mentioned she had purchased in Paris. Paris, for crying out loud! Barbara immediately became the trend-setter for the group. By the next bridge night, the following month, every woman in the room had emulated her look—with whatever they could get their hands on. Despite Gettysburg's new worldly residents, it was still a small town without huge demand for the latest fashions—the closest *en vogue* boutique was in Baltimore, 60 miles away, or in Washington and Philadelphia, a bit further afield— and Grace couldn't afford any of them. Not on her 1960 college professor's salary. Anyway, even if she had the money, she'd rather spend it on books, or a good bottle of gin.

It was getting close to noon at the GCC and the sun was blazing. The ladies were now lying tidily in a row, facing the pool and sipping their watery Cokes. Carol and Susan had since arrived. Lois watched her daughter curl her toes over the edge of the diving board, getting ready to jump off.

"Carol! Always wait until the person in front of you swims to the side before you jump…Okay, the coast is clear. Go!" Lois held her hand over her heart with relief as soon as Carol landed safely in the pool, 15 feet below. "The kids sure love that high dive. I wish they would stick to the lower diving board and spare me a heart attack."

"I know what you mean. Oh, look! There's Barbara." Jane laid down the scissors she was using to clip coupons out of her magazine and waved.

"Hi, ladies, sorry I'm late. I had a few errands to run, so I dropped off the girls for a bit." Barbara looked for the closest lounge chair to pull up. "I figured you would keep an eye on them. I hope that was all right?"

"Of course!" Lois got up to help Barbara carry a lounge chair over to Queens' Row—what the locals called this elite group of women, who were like a permanent fixture along the entrance to the club's pool. No one dared touch the chairs of Queens' Row without an explicit invitation.

"We have another White House function coming up this weekend. Would it be okay if Susan slept over at your place?" Barbara gave Lois a pleading smile as they set the chair down.

"Susan is such a sweetheart. She's welcome in our

home anytime. Carol told me the other day that Susan is her best friend." Lois said all of this a bit louder than necessary, hoping others entering the pool area might hear. "Isn't that the sweetest thing you ever heard?" She asked, clearly not expecting an answer.

"Would you look at the thighs on Ethel! Two o'clock!" Jane murmured under her breath. Grace looked up and quickly averted her eyes. "It's as if she stopped caring about what she looks like." Ethel Doyle was a fifth grade teacher at Meade School. She had a reputation for being strict with the children, washing out their mouths with soap if they said a bad word. Ethel liked to brag that she was Barbara Eisenhower's favorite local, as she had her son David in class.

"Oh, I know. Her swimsuit barely fits her rear end." Lois gave a little laugh.

"I don't know what you ladies have against Ethel," Barbara chimed in. "She's perfectly nice to me and my children."

Grace didn't contribute to the gossip today. She heard her friends' words, but it was as if they were talking underwater. She didn't care about Ethel's thighs. All she could think about was the potential life growing inside her. By her last calculation, the fetus was approximately five weeks old, roughly the size of a tadpole, or so she had read in a book at the college library. The past two nights since she'd seen her physician Dr. Weikert for a urine test, she'd lain in the bedroom next to Ed's, her husband of eleven years, paralyzed with fear, yet full of hope and wonder. It would take two weeks for the results to come back. So, two weeks of waiting. Two weeks of playing out every scenario imaginable. Two weeks of worry, dread, and excitement that grew with each day she failed to see her period. She'd begged Dr. Weikert to keep the news confidential and he assured her it was his job to do so. He assumed it was because she had to get used to the idea and he sympathized. After all, thirty-eight years old was significantly late for a baby, and, as he had made plain several times, "there could be complications." They scheduled an appointment for two weeks later to discuss the results.

Now here she was, sitting on Queens' Row and listening to her friends gossip about Ethel's thighs on a hot day in June. Grace wasn't a religious person, but now she found herself looking up to the plush white clouds, praying to God and asking him—or her—for a sign, for some direction as to what to do next.

Grace felt her skin sizzling under the midday sun as she watched a mother playing with her son in the pool. The boy must have been around two years old. The mother grabbed him under his armpits and swayed him gently through the water, creating small waves. The boy screamed with laughter, pure joy on his face. Grace found herself smiling too, until the word "motherhood" popped into her head. She cringed at it. What did it actually mean? The "hood" part made it sound like a special club, into which you'd need to be initiated. As if giving birth were the sole rite of passage into a magical world that only existed for those who were lucky, holy, and fertile enough.

She knew her friends probably wondered why she and Ed hadn't had kids, but luckily they'd never brought it up. It simply wasn't something you discussed openly. Could Grace ever call herself a mother? She knew what a mother was supposed to be, but her own mother leaving when she was thirteen had tarnished her reverence for the role.

Grace's mother had been absent from all her life milestones—getting her first period, her graduation, her wedding. Her mother had been depressed, trapped, not living the life she'd wanted for herself. So she left. Grace cried herself to sleep for months, but then she got angry. What kind of mother walks out on her children? What kind of wife walks out on her husband? She thought it best to block the event completely, throwing herself into the role of responsible older sister and respected daughter. The kind of woman who would never do such a thing. Grace had ultimately convinced herself that she would never be a mother, and that was okay. She had her cat, and she enjoyed watching her friends' children grow up before her eyes. Plus, she had ample time to read books, which was more than her friends with children could say. Imagine not having time to read a book! For the past decade, this had been how she'd made peace with being childless.

Lord knows she'd had to confront her childless existence and nurse her wounded pride regularly over the years. Like recently, at Lois's son's birthday party, when Grace had shown up with a copy of *Siddhartha*. Lois had laughed. "A book?! You really don't know children, do you, Grace?" Grace had been mortified and hurt when Lois laid it on the gift table where it later got buried under a mountain of wrapping paper. And the time when Jane got frustrated with Grace as they were trying to schedule a double date with their husbands. "Easy enough for you, Grace! You can go out whenever you please. I, on the other hand, have to taxi kids around to baseball practice, then gymnastics. I don't have a single night free this month."

True, she didn't know how to braid hair or which toys were popular, but she knew what it felt like the first time you saw your baby. When you smelled their sweet head, and how the folds under their chin felt all soft against your hands. But that was a secret no one knew, not even Ed. Her mother wasn't around to know. She didn't dare tell her father at the time. No, the secret and the shame that came along with it was hers alone, something she carried with her and hid like a precious stone or an ugly birthmark—depending on her mood.

Around 2:00 p.m. Grace called it a day at the country club. "Ladies, I'm off. I have papers to grade."

Lois looked up from her book. "Okay, dear. Will we see you at bridge club next Tuesday?"

"Yes, I'll be there." Grace packed up her things, holding her pool bag in front of her stomach. She felt lightheaded as she stood up, seeing a black starry fuzz for a second or two. Jane must have noticed. "Grace sweetie, are you okay?"

"Yes, just a bit dizzy there. Low blood pressure, I guess."

"Here, have a sip of my Coke, there's some left."

Grace took a small sip and slipped on her sandals.

When she reached her car in the parking lot, she placed her towel on the blazing hot seat and slid in behind the wheel. She let out a deep sigh of relief before putting her keys in the ignition. It felt like she had just passed a test. But really, her test had only just begun. In two weeks she would know for sure. And that was the strange thing about life, Grace had come to learn, a lot could happen in two weeks time.

Later that afternoon, as Jane drove herself home from the club, she remembered Jack saying they were out of toilet paper. She knew they were out of toothpaste and she could really use a new lipstick; it was down to a stub. G.C. Murphy, the local five-and-ten store, was on the way home. Not only could you buy 45 records, you could buy sewing notions and fabric, cosmetics, hardware, curtains, and candy.

Arthur was sticking price tags on the latest shipment of a fancy new face cream and placing them on the shelves when Jane arrived. Even Murphy's was feeling the town's fervor over its famous new residents. Anytime a magazine mentioned a product Mamie

Eisenhower used, requests from locals would start pouring in.

"Well good afternoon, Jane! Haven't seen you in here for a while. How's Jack?"

"Hi, Arthur. Jack's good—busy as always at the dealership. The newest model of the Chevy Impala just came out."

"Those are nice lookin' cars. Love the triple tail lights." Arthur continued sticking prices on products. "Let me know if you can't find anything."

"Thanks, Arthur, I will."

As she walked back to the toothpaste section, she saw the top of two heads in the next aisle over from her—one brunette, with hair in an updo, the other frizzy and blond.

"I heard she's been unhappy in her marriage for quite some time."

"Well, that would explain everything, wouldn't it?"

"Someone saw a man leave her house one afternoon."

"Can you imagine? The nerve! Sneaking around like that at her age."

Jane couldn't help but lean in closer, her face nearly touching the tubes of toothpaste lined up on the shelf.

Who on earth could they be talking about? She knew everyone, and everything, in Gettysburg—it was such a small town. But this was something she'd not even caught a whiff of. She leaned in even closer to catch the next bit of gossip, but the sound of toothpaste boxes hitting the floor made the women go quiet. The brunette woman stood on her tiptoes to see if she could spot the culprit. Jane quickly bent down to pick up the toothpaste boxes and hide from the woman's prying eyes.

The other woman asked her friend if she had everything she needed.

"I believe I do. Come on. Let's get out of here."

Jane peered over the aisle divider to see if she could make out the blond woman, but all she could see were two backs in summer dresses, walking toward the cash register. She gathered the other items she needed before heading over to the cashier herself. Small town gossip was commonplace. Jane, of all people, having grown up in Gettysburg, should know. Her mother always told her, "If you don't have anything nice to say about some-one, don't say anything at all." Jane had blown that one this morning with her comments about Ethel's thighs, but she couldn't help herself. For all the danger and damage gossip could cause, it was hard to resist.

2
MRS. Degree

September 1, 1940

The majority of women who attended Smith College went to obtain their MRS Degree and gain entry to the premier Ivy League marriage market. But not Grace. No, she was there because Smith was also known to have the best English literature program in the country. A whole course focused on the epics—Homer's *Iliad*, Virgil's *Aeneid*. An entire semester devoted to Virginia Woolf. She couldn't wait! Ever since sophomore year of high school, when her friend Shirley's mother, Mrs. Hamilton, had given her the idea that it was possible to have a career based solely around knowledge of literature, Grace had known she wanted to become an English professor. The weekend Mrs. Hamilton had taken her and Shirley to a Smith alumni event had been the best weekend of Grace's life so far, and the moment her future career path seemed to come into focus. She wasn't in the market for a Harvard man; although, sure, if she ended up meeting one, fine. Above all else, Grace wanted to be able to support herself financially and be better educated than her parents. She was in pursuit of greater opportunity and broader horizons. Mrs. Hamilton instilled this counter-culture ethos in her, perhaps knowing her own daughter couldn't live up to her expectations.

Now here she was, at Orientation Day at Smith. Grace's father, George, whistled a tune as they made their way through the sweet little town of Northampton, Massachusetts, after an almost two-hour drive from their hometown of Lowell, where Broadway ingénue Bette Davis had grown up. They made their way past the impressive Academy of Music Theatre to Elm Street and the gates of Smith College. It was a Sunday. Grace sat in the passenger seat of their Mercury Eight Town Sedan. Her brother Andrew was in the back, with his comic books. The trunk contained one large chest filled with her clothes, linens and, of course, her favorite books.

Her father glanced over at her. "Calvin Coolidge used to live here, ya know?"

"Yes Dad, I know." Grace adjusted her hair, using the side mirror of the car.

"And Sylvester..."

Grace cut him off, rolling her eyes. "And Sylvester Graham, who invented Graham Crackers. Yes dad. I know all the local celebrities. I did my research."

"Sure you did, sweetheart. I'm going to miss you, that's all. I guess I'm nervous." He reached over to grab her hand and squeezed it tight. Grace, realizing she was being snappy, squeezed back. In the six years since Grace's mother had walked out on them her father had remained single. Women would pursue him, bringing freshly baked goods to his door, but this was met with a disinterest that masked his fear of having his heart stomped on again. George counted himself a broken man, occasionally turning to the bottle when he wasn't able to sell his quota of Kirby Model C vacuum cleaners door-to-door.

"I'm going to miss you too, Dad. But I'm only two hours away. I'll try to come home on the weekends as much as possible to help with chores around the house."

"No, you just focus on your studies, honey. That's why we arranged for Thelma from next door to come over and help Andrew and me out more often. We'll be just fine."

"Okay, well, I left a couple of meals for you both in the freezer. And don't forget to put the empty milk bottles out on the porch every Monday for pick up."

"Honey, stop. We'll be fine. Just enjoy college. You deserve it."

Although Grace knew she deserved it, she couldn't help but feel guilty. Shirley's mom had helped her with her college application, and to secure a scholarship that covered the majority of her tuition. It was as if Mrs. Hamilton had quasi-adopted Grace; she always found ways big and small to serve as her academic advocate. Her own daughter was only interested in "boys, boys, boys". Mrs. Hamilton saw Grace as a sort of long-term project, a young lady she could help condition and mold into something strong, independent, and beautiful. Despite being grateful for all the attention, part of Grace still worried about what she was leaving behind. Andrew had a couple of difficult years of high school ahead of him. Who would protect him if he was bullied at school? Who would listen to his stories when he got home? Their father was always out selling his vacuum cleaners to eke out a living as more and more people started shopping at department stores. Thank God for their old neighbor, Thelma, who had agreed to cook meals and help out with the housekeeping. Grace had gotten used to being the only female in the household, and she knew it was an enormous responsibility to bear. She had done all the cooking and cleaning, and she had basically raised her brother Andrew. Grace just hoped that Thelma and the others would be patient with him. He had difficulty with social interactions and tended to fixate on just one thing. Andrew seemed to have come with an instruction manual only Grace could understand.

"Holy smokes, would you look at this?" George remarked as he pulled up in front of College Hall. "I've never seen anything like it. Only girls in every direction you look. Not a single guy."

Her father, uncomfortable and out of place, stayed in the car with Andrew while Grace made her way to the entrance where a line was forming for registration. A warm breeze riffled the acceptance letter in her hand. The noon sun shone brightly on the pristine green lawn, making her squint. Grace had fallen in love with the campus when she'd visited it with Shirley and Mrs. Hamilton. Beautiful old red-brick buildings. Paradise Pond, with its own boathouse, where the rowers raced at sunrise. And the library, with its beautiful neoclassical pillars and creeping ivy, erected in 1909 thanks to a donation from Andrew Carnegie. Like many liberal arts colleges, Smith had been inspired by the British university system, and placed its students in houses, which was also where they ate their meals. There were no sororities at Smith. Rather, Smith was one big sorority. That idea appealed to Grace. She didn't know anyone else attending Smith, but was excited to meet new people. She hadn't had much time for friends or extracurricular activities in high school.

As Grace waited in line, she sensed that the girl behind her was working up the nerve to talk to her. "Do you know your house assignment yet?"

"Pardon me?" Grace turned and saw a slender brunette with perfectly groomed eyebrows, wearing an eyelet blouse and red pleated skirt.

"Talbot," Grace replied shyly.

"Ah, just like me!"

"Well, it's nice to meet you! I'm Grace." Grace extended her hand.

"Hi, Grace! Nice to meet you, too. I'm Nancy." She gave a firm handshake, one Grace was not expecting from a girl with such a small frame. "I'm a bit nervous. Are you?"

"Yes. Yes, I am." Saying it out loud helped. Grace laughed. A relieved laugh.

"My mom always told me to think about one thing if I was nervous."

"What's that?"

"That there are only two things that are certain in life. We're all born, and we all die. No use wasting time on being nervous."

"Does that work for you?" Grace asked.

"No, not really. I'm nervous about the coursework, but I think most of these other girls are nervous about the mixers. I'm not interested in wasting all my time on boys."

"Me, neither!" Grace could tell they would get along just fine. There was something warm and light about Nancy. The way she held herself was strong and graceful. She was evidently someone who had self-confidence without being brash.

Once Grace got the keys to her room, she hopped back in the car with her dad and Andrew and they drove two blocks to Talbot House. Breaking a sweat, George and Andrew lugged Grace's chest up the stairs to her room. But the moment they stepped foot on the second floor, where Grace's room was, they were startled by a woman yelling, "Man on the floor!"

"What in the...?!" George looked down the hall—a middle-aged woman was walking toward him. She extended her hand.

"Sorry, I didn't mean to frighten you. That's just

one of our house rules. As soon as a man is on the floor, we have to inform everyone. Welcome. You must be Grace's father, and brother, I presume." She smiled at Andrew, who was almost as tall as George. "I'm Ms. Halloway, Talbot's housemother."

"Nice to meet you, Ms. Halloway." George shook her hand. "Do you live in this house with the students?"

"Yes. Each house has its own housemother. I have a small apartment on the top floor." While they chatted, Grace stepped into her room and discovered that her window overlooked the library. Rapping twice with her knuckle on the open door, Ms. Halloway led the men into her room. "And you must be Grace. Welcome!" Grace was not sure whether to curtsy or shake hands. She chose the latter.

"Good day, ma'am."

"You can call me Ms. Halloway. I hope you'll find your room comfortable. You know, you have the best view," she said with a wink. "I'll let you get settled. Dinner is downstairs at 7:00 p.m. Skirts are required. I'll go over all the house rules with you ladies this evening. For now, I'll leave you to it." Ms. Halloway gave them all a smile before going downstairs.

George and Andrew picked up Grace's chest from the hallway and carried it into her room, setting it by the foot of her bed. Grace leaned out her window and inhaled the fresh air.

"Isn't this gorgeous, Dad?!"

"It sure is, honey. You're one lucky gal. Look, Grace, your brother and I should get on the road. Plus, we don't want to be in your way. Looks like you have a lot of unpacking to do and a busy night ahead of you." George looked down and wiped his forehead with a handkerchief.

"Are you sure you don't want to stay a bit longer? You're welcome to. We can grab a bite to eat in town. You haven't even had lunch."

George hung his head. "No, Grace, it's fine. You know how I hate goodbyes, so let's just get it over with. We'll stop somewhere on the way home for lunch."

Grace felt a deep pit of sadness and guilt at her core. Now two women had left this man. It was almost too much to bear. Grace went to her father. She held him tight and could feel him trembling. He was a good head taller than her, and she nestled her head in his neck. The familiar smell of his aftershave gave her comfort, but made saying goodbye much more difficult. She turned to face Andrew, who was sitting on her bed and looking down toward the floor. He hadn't said much all day, and only when spoken to.

"Oh, Andrew. I am going to miss you so, so much." Grace plunked down beside him, looping her arm around him for a tight squeeze. Andrew kept his head down and Grace saw a teardrop fall to the floor. "Hey buddy, don't cry. You're breaking my heart. I'm only two hours away. There's a bus that goes from Lowell to Northampton. You can come visit anytime, okay?"

Andrew nodded and wiped his eyes with his sleeve. He turned toward his big sister and buried his head in her shoulder. Grace and Andrew had always had a special bond. She understood him, when the rest of the world seemed incapable of it. She thought back to a day in church, years ago, when Ms. Reber had whispered, "He's not 100 percent there, is he?" to her husband, because Andrew had failed to make eye contact after greeting her. He was just a child! Grace sometimes felt like strangling small-minded people like that.

Grace appreciated Andrew's gentle way, and his fixation on astrology. The stars had always been his escape when their parents argued. For Grace, it had been books from the library and using her imagination.

She thought back to the morning her mother left them, two weeks before Christmas. She was thirteen, her brother was eight. She'd just helped him pick out a warm outfit for school. When they made their way down the stairs they heard a plate break on the floor and her parents screaming. She covered Andrew's ears as they waited in the hall leading to the kitchen, where the fighting was taking place. She remembered seeing her mother's leather suitcase through the crack in the door. The back door slammed. That was that.

"I will survive" was the motto Grace had come to live by. It crashed in on her when suddenly there was no one to cook, or to care for her, her brother, and her dad. She took it all upon herself, because who else would? It was expected of her, but she also did it because she loved them both so much. In her book, they had done nothing wrong. Her father showed his love through butterfly kisses and teaching her how to whistle. She and Andrew always had fun together, despite their age difference of five years. They would build a fort out of the cushions on the couch, and she would tell him ghost stories or start tickle fights.

Now she was worried about them as they left her dorm room. Guilt weighed on her like a ton of bricks. But she had to survive. She was eighteen years old now; a woman. It was her turn to make something of her life. But she felt blocked from fully enjoying the moment.

"Come on, buddy! Let's get on the road." George grabbed Andrew's hand. "We'll let Grace get settled. Call us when you get a chance, okay, hon?"

"I will, Dad. I promise." She watched as they walked out of her room and down the hall. She moved to the window and watched as they got in the car. They honked, waved up at her, then drove away. They were still waving as they rounded the corner. She waved back. "I love you!" she yelled out the window.

Weeks passed. A fall chill arrived on campus and leaves began changing color, to fiery oranges and reds. Grace reveled in her college routine and studies. She started keeping a journal. On the first page she wrote about how, for the first time in her life, she felt she was in her element, like she belonged. She was always up by 8:00 a.m for a breakfast of porridge in the Talbot dining room, then it was off to a day full of lectures and learning. She devoured books, becoming completely absorbed in them. Nancy managed to drag her away from time to time, for a walk around campus or ice cream in town, but every moment she wasn't in class, Grace was in the library. Her favorite desk was on the ground floor, in front of a large window. She'd usually bring an apple, or something else to stop her stomach from growling between meals. She'd open up her rucksack, turn on the green desk lamp, and read. Books on transcendentalism, by Henry David Thoreau and Ralph Waldo Emerson, fascinated her. The idea that people are at their best when they are self-reliant and independent. But her favorite book by far was Ayn Rand's *We the Living*. She had read it three times that first semester of her freshman year. Grace could relate to the protagonist's free spirit and strong will and saw parallels in their stories: Kira Argounova going off to technical school, Grace going off to Smith. Both girls had faced hard circumstances at home, but had overcome them through determination.

She checked in with Andrew and her father each week, usually on Sundays, just after breakfast. They never had much to report, although one time Andrew was very eager to update her on a new star that had been discovered. Her dad was doing more demos of the Kirby Model C, hoping to save up money to buy some good gifts that Christmas. She told them all about her classes and the books she had been reading. Her father feigned excitement the best he could, for her benefit—"Wow, that's great, honey!" — but she could hear him yawning on the other end of the line. That was okay; she didn't expect either of them to understand college life. Her dad hadn't been to college himself. All the more reason for Grace to appreciate every moment. No matter how much she resented her, she knew her mother would have wanted her to follow her dreams. After all, that's why her mother had left in the first place, because she felt trapped and unable to follow her own path. If only her mother could see her now.

There were mixers at Smith almost every weekend, each time with a different school—Dartmouth, Amherst, Yale, Harvard. Each house would take turns hosting the parties in their first-floor common space, during which young men could go upstairs and visit with the women. But there were three rules each house had to follow:

1. The door had to be open and the window shades had to be up;

2. Three feet must be kept on the ground at all times. So if a couple was sitting on a bed, three out of their four feet had to be on the ground; and

3. When a man entered the upstairs area, you had to yell "man on the floor!"—a rule the Gilmartins had learned quickly on arrival day.

Grace hadn't had much interest in these mixers her first two years. Boys distracted her from focusing on her studies. Plus, having witnessed her parents' marriage fall apart, all the arguing and her mother's tears, she'd decided she didn't want that for herself.

As the years without word from her mother—Margie—passed by, Grace had stopped wondering whether the situation was permanent. And if she was honest with herself, she was relieved that it was permanent. Her parents had always argued. Sometimes it was about dinner being too cold, or George's shirts not being pressed to his liking. But nine times out of ten it was about how George had snatched Margie out of the life she was *supposed* to have lived. She had been on track to become a professional dancer in New York City, where they had met. When Grace was very young, her mother would regale her with stories about the rehearsals, parties, and shows, leaving her daughter wide-eyed and eager to hear more. Grace remembered watching her mother applying lipstick one night, preparing to go out and hear a Big Band concert with her father. George had yelled at Margie from downstairs to hurry up. Margie jumped and smeared her lipstick across her face. She threw the lipstick at the mirror, cracking the glass. "I'm already too late,

George," she screamed, then turned toward Grace with a sense of urgency. "Never, and I mean *never*, give up on your dreams, Grace. Promise me that?" Ever since that night, and especially after her mother had left, Grace had kept that promise. She was going to have a better life than her mother had had. Being better educated was a good start. She didn't want to lose her scholarship or her independence, so she kept her nose in her books.

Grace wasn't really interested in any of the young men she met until one night, at the first mixer of her junior year in the fall of 1942. The mandatory mixers always started out the same, no matter which school the guests were from. This particular week there was a group of young men from Amherst. Non-alcoholic drinks were served in the parlor, then everyone moved to the dining room for a formal dinner followed by dancing—or by socializing upstairs, with the doors open and three feet on the ground, of course. Bored to tears, and annoyed because she wanted to read, Grace went to fill Nancy's glass and her own with spiked punch. When she looked up, she met the dark eyes of a young man standing a few feet away from her by the piano. He smiled, then turned his attention back to the three other men he was standing with, all the while watching Grace out of the corner of his eye as she returned to her group of friends. Grace felt butterflies flutter in her stomach.

"What are you smiling about?" Nancy asked, when Grace returned with their drinks.

"Oh, nothing." Grace looked down at the ground, trying to hide her smile, but she couldn't help herself and snuck a glance at the group of men standing by the piano. Nancy followed Grace's eyes.

"Oh, I see." Nancy nudged Grace with her elbow. "You better look out for him, though. That's Peter Bowers, the so-called 'Cat of Amherst.' Every girl would give her right arm to be with him, and he knows it."

Ms. Halloway tapped a glass with her knife. "Dinner is served."

The young men and women made their way to the dining room. Grace went straight for a chair at the center of the table. She had learned after a few of these dinners never to sit at the *end* of the table, because if the conversation was dull there would be no escape. When you sat in the middle, you had more people to talk to. Seating was not assigned, but you did have to sit boy-girl-boy-girl. After all, it was a mixer.

To Grace's surprise, the man with dark eyes and hair appeared behind her and pulled out her chair for her.

"Let me help you with that," he said. "I'm Peter." Now getting a closer look, Grace took note of how handsome his face was, and how tall he was. "Do you mind if I sit across from you?" There were dimples near his mouth when he smiled, and a mole on his cheek.

"I'm Grace. Nice to meet you." Her face flushed and her heart started beating wildly. She couldn't believe it. Could this be how Kira Argounova felt when she met Leo Kovalensky, the aristocratic and brilliant young scholar with whom she fell in love at first sight, in *We the Living*? It was as if no one else in the room existed. Their eyes were locked on each other throughout dinner. Their conversation flowed like water. She laughed at all his jokes and impersonations of movie stars, because she genuinely thought they were funny. And he laughed at hers.

Grace learned that Peter was from Boston. He was the youngest of four siblings and the only boy. Could that be why he was such a charmer, growing up with so many sisters? His father was a banker, his mother a socialite. He played rugby and liked poetry. He was studying political science and law. His dream was to be an

FBI agent, or to work for the OSS. He was inquisitive, asking Grace about her future, her dreams. She didn't give him too many details, as she didn't want to bore him. There wasn't much to tell, really. She was third generation Irish from an industrial town in Massachusetts. She had a salesman father, a mother who had left the family, and a younger brother who was obsessed with astrology. Not exactly seductive conversation material.

After dinner, Grace offered Peter a peppermint she had in her pocket.

He popped it in his mouth. "Ah-choo. Ah-choo. Ahhh-choo!" He sneezed three times, in quick succession. Grace laughed and shook her head.

"My, my, are you okay there?"

"Pardon me, yes. I always sneeze with peppermint—and red wine—for some reason."

Grace found this made him even more endearing. She looked over at Nancy, who mouthed to her, "Oh, my God!" Grace smiled and pretended not to notice as she invited Peter up to her room. She felt the other boys and girls staring as they walked toward the stairs. A majority of her housemates remained downstairs, playing cards with the Amherst boys and listening to music.

"Man on the floor!" Grace called as she led him into her room. Peter walked over to the photographs

Grace had framed on her dresser. "Mind if I have a look?"

"No, of course not."

"This must be Andrew. And is this your father?"

"Yes, it's an old photo, but that's them."

"And this must be your mother? She's beautiful! Now I see where you get it." He winked and held up the photo next to Grace. She felt her face go red.

"Have a seat," Grace said, as she motioned toward her desk. Peter sat on her chair, Grace on her bed. At that moment Ms. Halloway peered in.

"Everything okay in here? Shades up? Good. Okay, you two, keep this door open, three feet on the floor."

Grace nodded and smiled. "Yes, Ms. Halloway." Ms. Halloway continued down the hall and down the stairs.

"Hey, what do you say we take a little walk?" Peter suggested.

"But that's not allowed."

"I know, but no one has to know. Our bus back to Amherst doesn't leave until 11 p.m. There has to be a way out of here, where no one will see us. I need to walk off all that food."

"Well, there is a fire escape down the hall," Grace offered. "But what if we get caught?"

"Don't worry, I'll take the blame. Come on, before your housemother gets back." Peter took Grace's hand and she grabbed a cardigan from a hook. She peered to the left and right, then led Peter out of her room and down the hall to the window leading to the fire escape. Peter went first, then motioned to Grace that the coast was clear. She hurried out the window, then thought she heard someone coming. She held her breath for a second, ducking down low on the landing. After the voices faded, she continued climbing down the ladder. When she got to the end, she realized that she would have to jump several feet to the ground. She looked below and Peter was standing there with his arms wide open. She fretted that he might see up her skirt.

"Come on! Hurry! Jump! I'll catch you. I promise!" Peter hissed.

Grace jumped into his arms. His minty breath enveloped her, as did the smell of his skin, which was fresh and warm, like sandalwood soap.

He grabbed her hand and whispered, "Come on. Let's go! Quick!" They jogged along the back of the house, toward Paradise Pond. The moon was bright, casting white ripples on the water. Once they got to the boathouse they burst out laughing and stopped to catch their breath.

Peter looked at Grace, Grace at Peter. After staring in each other's eyes for what felt like an eternity, he leaned in and kissed her. Grace gave into it completely. She had only kissed two other boys in her life and this one easily beat out the others. Peter's lips were so soft, she felt herself melting into them. Before she knew it, they were undressing and moving into the boathouse. Peter broke away and threw a couple of outdoor cushions and woolen blankets on the ground, then he pulled Grace back toward him. "Come, sit here." Grace had no objections. They continued undressing each other, and threw their shoes off to the side. It was still comfortably warm for September.

Grace was still a virgin but, based on the stories she'd heard from her friends, it was about time. She liked Peter. She liked him a lot, actually. So why the hell not sleep with him? She was twenty for Christ's sake! He asked her if she was comfortable, if she was okay with what they were doing. She told him to shut up and make love to her. It hurt a bit at first, but he was gentle and affectionate. Afterwards, they lay in each other's arms, listening to the boats outside rocking on the water. He pointed out Orion and the Big Dipper. She thought about how well he would get along with her brother.

"I've never met a girl like you before, Grace." Peter kissed her on her cheek.

"How do you mean?"

"For starters, you're the most beautiful person I've ever seen. But you're intelligent, witty, and you have this fire inside you. I can't explain it." He smiled and pulled the blanket over their bodies.

"Well, you're not so bad yourself." Grace nuzzled her head on his chest. They stayed there for at least another half hour, talking, until Grace looked at her watch and saw that it was 10:30. "Come on, we have to get dressed and get you back!" Grace said in a panic. "It would be so embarrassing if you were left here. And God forbid Ms. Halloway is looking for us!"

When they returned to Talbot House, Peter lifted her up to reach the fire escape. The window was still open. Grace went in first, carefully looking left and right to make sure no one was in the hall. She heard laughter coming from downstairs, where card games were still being played. She heard Ms. Halloway's voice and, to her great relief, it sounded like she was playing cards, too. Grace signaled to Peter that the coast was clear to follow her. Back in her room, she quickly looked in the mirror, making sure her lipstick wasn't smudged and her hair wasn't too wild. While she was checking her appearance, Peter wrote something on a piece of paper at her desk.

Grace turned around. "What are you writing?"

"My address and our house phone number. Grace, please promise me you'll write, or call."

"Okay, I promise." At that moment Ms. Halloway rang a bell indicating that it was time for everyone to say their goodbyes. The bus for the Amherst boys had pulled up out front. Grace and Peter walked downstairs, hand in hand. Nancy noticed this and winked at Grace. Grace winked back.

On the porch, Peter pulled Grace close and whispered in her ear, "I've fallen for you, Grace," and he kissed her cheek. Grace blushed and smiled. Never before had she felt like this. Perhaps the closest comparison would be the feeling of flying, although she had only experienced that in her dreams. Their eyes were glued to each other as he walked to the bus and disappeared into the darkness once on board. She heard one of his buddies ask him where he had been, but she didn't hear his answer. That night, Grace wasn't able to sleep a wink. All she could do was think of Peter. She'd fallen for him, too. Hard.

◆◆◆

She had always been a bit irregular, but when her period was three weeks late, she began to worry. Her breasts were hurting, and she felt different. It was the end of October 1942, and Halloween was approaching. Smith College had a wonderful nurse at the infirmary named Ruth who was like a mother figure to the young women on campus. Grace made an appointment with Ruth after confiding in Nancy about her late period. It was Nancy who had suggested she might in fact be pregnant. The word "pregnant" alone shocked her. She had only had sex once in her life! She was a straight-A student with plans to attend graduate school—she was young, with a whole life to live.

The wind was howling outside and rain pattered against the window as Grace sat opposite Ruth at the infirmary.

Ruth leaned across her desk, her eyes soft. "What brings you here today, Grace? I haven't seen you since you had strep throat last winter, you poor thing."

"My period is late. I'm afraid I might be..." Grace started shaking in her chair and swallowed the lump in her throat.

"Are you sexually active?" Ruth asked matter-of-factly.

"No, I mean, well, yes... I had sex once. My first

time actually, at the fall mixer. How could I have been so st—."

"Now, stop right there. You are *not* stupid, Grace. Believe me, you're not the first girl to come in here with this issue."

"I'm not?" Grace sat up straight in her chair. Ruth handed her a tissue.

"Of course not. Honey, this is a girls' college. Now listen, if you are indeed pregnant—and we'll do a blood test to find out—you have a couple of options."

Grace listened intently, squeezing her hands together as Ruth laid everything out for her. Molex pills had been deemed unsafe two years ago. Abortions were illegal in every state. There were some exceptions, and backstreet abortions could be arranged, but not without serious risk. The best option, in Ruth's opinion, was to go to a maternity home. She knew of two in particular that might be good fits in Grace's case. One was a small facility in upstate New York, right on the Finger Lakes. The other was slightly larger, Catholic, and located in Dorchester, on the outskirts of Boston, just two hours away.

Grace gazed at Ruth like she was an oracle, as the nurse continued with her advice. "What you could do is say that you're going to study abroad for a semester.

Normally, we would be sending students to Paris in the spring. But because of the war, we have a faculty-led program going to Quebec this year. I know it sounds like a long shot, but this will buy you enough time, allowing you to continue with your studies." The more Ruth talked about it, the more animated she became. "I can maybe get a couple of professors to work with me on this one. Have your baby, and no one will ever have to know." Ruth grabbed Grace's hand from across the desk. "I've done this sort of thing before."

Grace was stuck on the words "your baby." It hadn't quite sunken in yet. She felt too young and inexperienced to be a mother. She had never even babysat a child, except for her own brother. She let Ruth's plan land. "What happens at the end?"

"When you say 'the end', do you mean after you have the baby?" Ruth smiled.

"Yes."

"The baby is put up for adoption—matched with a family."

Grace sat there for a moment in silence, taking it all in. A chill ran through her and she buttoned her cardigan up all the way. "How much will that cost?"

"Well, I don't know the exact figure, but somewhere around $100. It depends on whether you have a shared room or a single."

Grace gasped. "Who is going to pay for it?"

"Perhaps your father…"

Grace shook her head.

"Can I pour you a cup of tea, Grace?"

"Yes, please."

Ruth set a steaming cup of tea in front of Grace. "It's Lady Grey, hope that's okay." Ruth leaned back in her chair. "I might have an idea. A while back, the family of one of the girls I helped set up a fund—in gratitude—to help smart young women like yourself, who found themselves in the same position as their daughter but didn't have the resources to pay for it. This fund was set up discreetly, and is administered by me under the guise of a study abroad scholarship so they don't have to skip a beat in school and finish their degrees." Grace sat in silence, absorbing all of this new information. She stared out the window, watching the tree branches shed their leaves in the wind. The sky was dark and stormy. Thick clouds moved steadily overhead. She wondered whether this whole ordeal would set her back. She wanted to go to graduate school. She thought about her father, and Andrew, who was now fifteen and in high school. She probably wouldn't be showing by Christmas. She could spend the holidays with them before heading off to one of these clandestine "homes." There's no way she could let her father know. He would be so disappointed in her. She also felt sorry for him. He had endured enough. It had always been a struggle to put food on the table for his own two children, let alone having to worry about an extra mouth to feed.

She did the math in her head. The baby would be born by the end of June. She would be on summer break and all would be back to normal by the time her senior year started in the fall. The timing couldn't be better, actually. She felt a deep sense of relief at this idea alone. And with the news about the special fund that might be available to her, she felt a glimmer of hope that she could pull this off.

Nurse Ruth broke the silence, as if she could read Grace's mind. "Let's do a blood test today. That way we'll know definitively."

"How long does it take to get the results?"

"About two to three weeks. Once we know for sure, we can get you set up with your study abroad program," Ruth said with a warm smile. "And if you get your period in the meantime, you just let me know."

Later that evening, in Nancy's room, Grace found herself glancing around nervously as she worked up the courage to discuss her plan. The window was open slightly, making the sheer curtains dance. There was a photograph on Nancy's dresser of her and her mother at the beach. They were both sitting on the sand, Nancy's head resting on her mother's shoulder, both wearing big white smiles. Nancy caught Grace staring at the photo.

"That's me and my mom in Cape Cod. We go each summer together, for a week. Our family has a cottage there."

"Looks like fun." Grace felt a punch of jealousy.

Nancy stiffened as she realized her insensitivity. "I'm sorry, Grace. Did your mother ever write to you after she left? Have you ever gone looking for her?" Grace continued to stare at the photo. "Forget I asked! We don't have to talk about it," Nancy said as she walked over and closed the window.

"No. It's okay. I never really had anyone that I could talk to about it." Grace sat on the foot of Nancy's bed. "My summers were filled with household chores, cooking, and taking Andrew to baseball practice. When my mom left, I became the head of household. We didn't have enough time or money to go on a vacation together. Maybe vacations were too painful for my father.

Maybe they reminded him that his family was incomplete." Grace grabbed a pillow and hugged it as tears filled her eyes. Nancy sat down beside her, placing an arm around her. "I looked in the mailbox every single day for two years, waiting and hoping. Then one day I decided to stop torturing myself. She wasn't coming back. She didn't care about me. About us. Everyone was right about her. She was selfish."

"I'm so sorry, Grace. That must have been so hard."

"It was, to tell you the truth. After my mom left, the house seemed like it was in a perpetual fog. No laughter. No fun. Even the furniture seemed drab. Books were my only escape; I took mini vacations within their pages."

"And look at you now! Look at us, college girls. You did that, Grace. You got yourself into college. We're not going to let anyone take that away from you!" Nancy looked Grace straight in the eyes. "You hear me, Flopsy?" Nancy and Grace had made up nicknames for each other during freshman year.

"Yes. I hear you, Mopsy." Grace wanted to believe her. She really did. That's when Grace told her about what had happened with Peter. And "the plan." Nancy was on board, 100 percent.

♠♠♠

Grace did not get her period. Two weeks came and went and, with each day that passed, Grace grew more scared. She felt like a failure. How could she have let this happen? She went to get her results at the nurse's office. Ruth was nothing but supportive, walking Grace through all the steps that needed to happen—registering for a bed at the maternity home and buying a bus ticket, and finally, packing loose-fitting clothing to accommodate her growing body and some extra French language material so it looked like she'd actually learned something while she was "in Quebec." Grace asked Ruth not to tell her father, or anyone except Nancy, who'd offered to help with the logistics on campus. Ruth reminded Grace that she was an adult and therefore able to sign her own papers. They decided it was best to go with the slightly larger maternity home facility—the Catholic one, two hours away. The proximity would make it easier to get coursework to Grace, so she didn't have to skip a semester.

Grace stewed over whether she should tell Peter that she was pregnant. They had met up a couple of times since their first encounter, once for a football game, and once to see *The Road to Morocco*, followed by an ice cream sundae. But it was through letters to each other that they shared the most intimate details about their dreams for the future, what they wanted out of life. Grace told him all about her mother leaving and how she had her heart set on becoming a college professor. Peter talked about wanting to make his father proud of him, being the only son. They had fun together—he was always the perfect gentleman, giving her his jacket when she was cold, sending her flowers, and asking how her studies were going. They were smitten with each other. She weighed all the pros and cons and practiced various ways of telling him the news in front of the mirror. But what good would it do? She wasn't going to keep the baby; that much she knew. A baby didn't fit into her post-Smith academic plan. She knew what it was like to have her hands full at home with her own brother and her father. There was no way she could live in her own childhood home with a baby as well. According to the radio, America's young men were being drafted and sent overseas daily. Chances were, Peter would also be sent off to serve in the war, which showed no signs of flagging.

In early December there was another mixer with Amherst. Grace knew it could be the last time she'd see Peter for a while, maybe ever. She didn't want to ruin what they had by telling him about the pregnancy, especially when she truly thought they might end up together after the war. But the biggest red flag, the thing that kept her from telling him the most, was his recent reaction to the news that his roommate had gotten a girl pregnant. He wrote in a letter to Grace, "Can you imagine how horrible that would be? Basically your whole life, ruined—one big blockade. Poor guy!" And that was that. She couldn't risk springing the news on him if he couldn't even handle it happening to someone else. There were so many obstacles getting in the way of them being together already. Peter was graduating in May, men were being drafted, she was off to a maternity home. Even so, if it was meant to be, it would be, Grace thought. They would stay in touch through letters.

The night of the mixer, Grace was quieter than usual. She and Peter were cuddled under a wool blanket on the porch swing of Talbot House, his arm wrapped around her. "Grace, is something wrong?" Peter asked.

"I'm going to miss you, that's all." Tears welled in her eyes. Peter wiped them away with his thumbs and took her face into his hands.

"Look at me, Grace. You're the only girl for me, you hear? You're going off to Quebec for a semester. You'll be back before you know it. After graduation,

I'm going to apply where I can—the FBI, the OSS, anywhere that will take me if the draft doesn't whisk me away. I can come and visit you your senior year. Maybe you can go to grad school in Washington. What I'm saying is, it will all work out. For now, we'll just have to keep on writing letters." He kissed her forehead.

"You're right. That's all we can do." Grace smiled. "But what if you're drafted?"

"We'll find each other somehow, Grace Gilmartin." Peter reached into the pocket of his jacket and pulled out a small box. "I want you to have this. It was my mother's and she said that if I ever met a girl worthy of my heart, I should give it to her."

Grace, caught off guard, took the box and opened it. Inside was a delicate gold watch with a small round face. She couldn't believe it. Never before had she received such a special gift. "It's beautiful! I don't know what to say...I..." Peter placed the watch on her wrist, clasping it tightly. "I love it," Grace said, looking down at her new adornment, "Thank you."

"Now you have something to always remember me by." Peter smiled and held her hands in his. "We'll be back together before you know it."

And she believed him.

As Christmas break approached, Grace packed her

bags and prepared to say goodbye to her housemates. *Québec, j'arrive!*

Only Nancy knew where she was really going and Grace made her promise not to tell a soul. Nancy was her link back to campus, and she'd agreed to mail her coursework to her each week. The day after Christmas, which Grace spent with her father and brother, Nancy brought Grace to the local bus station. Grace wasn't showing yet, but had packed plenty of loose blouses. They both shivered as sleet fell from a gray sky.

"I'm so scared, Nancy." Grace said as she boarded the bus, suitcase in hand. There was a line of people bundled up in woolen coats waiting behind her.

"You comin' or not, young lady?" The bus driver shouted.

"It'll be okay, Grace. You're doing the right thing. This will all be over before you know it." Nancy gave her a big, warm sisterly hug. Grace climbed into the bus, handed the driver her ticket, and sat down in the back row. She held her hand up against the steamy window, feeling grateful she had Nancy, knowing that not all women could keep a secret well, especially one like this. A tear ran down her cheek. Nancy stood waving in the sleet, and she kept waving until the bus rounded the corner.

3

Studying Abroad at the Maternity Home

January 20, 1943

Grace always began her letters to her father and brother with *Bonjour*. She was surprised by her ability to make it seem like she really was studying abroad in Quebec. She had even made up a name for the tour guide who'd supposedly showed her around the magnificent Notre Dame.

The days are so much shorter here in winter. Oh dad, you thought Massachusetts was cold. There was ice today on the St. Lawrence River!

In reality, she was incredibly lonely at St. Mary's Maternity Home for unwed mothers. The nurses were strict. In their eyes, Grace had sinned and in order to repent she must scrub floors. An eerie silence lingered, as the girls in the home were not supposed to talk to each other. She filled her days with coursework and spent her evenings writing in her journal. While lying in bed at night, she fantasized about ways to escape. The food was delivered in a large truck every Tuesday. Maybe she could sneak in the back while they were unloading, but then where would she go? She wanted her life with her friends at Smith back. She was trapped. And suffocating.

After a few weeks there, out of desperation, or fear, or both, Grace felt a deep urge to tell Peter about the pregnancy, about their baby that would eventually go to parents who were not them. She thought that if she told him he might come pick her up and they could run off together. But each time she tried to imagine how that would play out, she concluded that it wasn't worth the risk. Even though she was head-over-heels about him, the reality was that they had only known each other for six months. Instead, she forced herself to compartmentalize her thoughts, a skill she'd acquired after her mother left as a coping mechanism. She used her journal as a home for her sacred, secret thoughts.

The baby is a Gemini. I read that Geminis are playful and curious.

Plus, she knew that there was no use telling Peter. He'd made it quite clear that marriage and children did not feature in his foreseeable future. He was on a path to serving his country, as a soldier or spy, not to being a family man. She was on a path to teaching what she loved and having a secure and independent life as a college professor. She kept her letters to Peter brief and light, writing about the porridge she had for breakfast, or the lumpy mattress she slept on. She sent her letters back to campus via an intercollegiate pouch, so Nancy could pass them on to Amherst, and Peter would not question the absence of international postage stamps. But no letters came back from him with her coursework. Just a small note from Nancy which read,

Sorry Grace, no news from Peter. He was probably drafted. Most of the boys I know have been.

Even though it was forbidden, the girls at the maternity home found ways to talk to each other, especially right before lights out, when the nurse on duty tended to slip away for a cup of tea. Some of the other girls had shared their stories with her, and all of them sounded much more complicated and intense than hers. There was a 15-year-old who'd been raped by her teacher. And a 17-year-old whose father had threatened to kill her if she ever dated someone outside her race, yet here she was pregnant by her black boyfriend.

"Don't you ever wish," Grace whispered one night to a girl in the bed next to hers, "that you could get out of here?"

"No. Where would I go? We're branded now Grace, 'fallen women,' 'whores.' I'd rather stay in here and get this baby out of me." The girl turned onto her back and looked up at the ceiling. "Anyways, it doesn't matter what I want; this is what my parents want." After a long silence, she continued, "You've got this all wrong, Grace. You think you have a choice. None of us have a choice."

Grace awoke the next morning with a headache. She found herself thinking a lot about her own mother, wondering how she would have responded to her own daughter's pregnancy. She sometimes imagined that she would have been secretly pleased. She remembered how her mother would stop at every stroller they passed by, peeking inside and asking questions of the mother, like, "Does he sleep through the night yet?" or "What a cutie, can I pinch those cheeks?" How would things be different now, if her mother had stuck around? Would Grace have kept the baby if she could've counted on her own mother willing and able to help her care for it? *It*—she didn't know whether the baby would be a girl or a boy. She had to force herself to be indifferent to avoid getting too attached to any ideas about what the child would be like. She wasn't going to raise this baby. Someone else would, and then she could go back to her normal life as a college student at Smith and pursue her dreams as she had always promised herself—and her mother—she would.

Was this desire not to be a mother deeply ingrained in her? Her mother had left her, now here she was about to do the same thing, even earlier on in her child's life. Her baby might end up feeling just as abandoned as she did. Or, was it simply that she wasn't ready to be a mother *right now*? This was the right order of things, she thought: graduate school, marriage to Peter, a job as a college professor, a house with a white picket fence, *then* children. She wrestled with these moral quandaries every day, and the internal struggle found its way into her subconscious at night. At one point she began having the most horrifying recurring dream. She was standing in a river, holding her newborn baby under the rushing water while it reached out for her with a look of terror and helplessness on its face.

One morning in late May Grace received a package from Nancy and took it straight to her room. Her roommate had given birth the week prior, so she had the space all to herself. The package contained her final coursework for the semester, but it felt heavier than usual. Inside, Grace was pleased to find a copy of Ayn Rand's The Fountainhead, which had just come out. There was also a letter from Nancy. She flipped over the envelope to open it and noticed a message scrawled in Nancy's handwriting:

Make sure you're sitting down when you read this!

She unfolded the letter, slowly lowered herself down onto her bed, and began reading.

Dear Grace,
How are you, my dear friend? I think of you daily.
I've missed our walks to town.
You'll be out of there soon enough. I thought this book might help you get through your last month. I have some difficult news to share and wanted to be the first to tell you.
I heard rumors that Peter died in the war. A girl from Talbot House, who is dating a young man

from Amherst, said no one has heard from him since he left. I hope it's not true, but it would explain why there have been no letters. I'm so sorry, Grace. I wish I was there to give you a hug. I know you loved him.

Hang in there, Flopsy!

Love,

Nancy

Grace held the letter against her chest and started rocking back and forth, cradling it like a baby. Tears ran down her cheeks and her heart swelled with pain. She felt cursed; first her mother, then the only man she'd ever loved. What had she done to deserve this? She curled up on her bed and cried into her pillow so that no one could hear her sobs.

Thank God for literature. She buried herself in the book Nancy had sent her, and didn't come out of her room for the entire day. A nurse came by and knocked once in the morning, and again in the afternoon. Grace sent her away, explaining that she wasn't feeling well and needed to rest. A book had come to her rescue once again. Books had been her escape during her parents' arguments, and now they were an escape from the dreadful maternity home and the painful news about Peter. Books let her step into a different world, a different life. A life that was not defined by loss.

After dinner one evening in early June, as she was helping with the dishes, Grace felt a warm trickle run down her leg. Despite living in an institution whose sole purpose was to facilitate childbirth, the girls there weren't given much information about the matter. The wet sensation caught Grace so off guard that she dropped the plate she'd been drying, which shattered on the tile floor.

"Grace! Are you okay?" Rachel, one of the girls who had arrived a month after Grace, started picking up the broken pieces with a dustpan.

"I don't know." Grace looked at the small puddle beneath her.

"Oh, boy! Okay. Stay right here. I'll go get one of the nurses."

Grace looked around for a towel to mop up the floor. A few moments later a middle-aged woman with mouse-brown hair rushed in and took Grace firmly by the arm.

"Come with me, dear. I'll take you to the delivery ward."

Grace felt a sudden sense of panic. She had heard stories from the other girls about how much childbirth hurt. That, coupled with the fact that she'd only seen the aftermath—girls who had just given their babies up for adoption looking as if their souls had been sucked out of them. They were only given a couple of days to recover, before being sent back to where they had come from, pale, exhausted, and empty-handed.

The nurse handed Grace a hospital gown that was open at the back, and big woolen socks.

"Put these on. You can change over there behind that curtain."

Grace walked over to the corner of the sterile room. The tiled floor felt cold on her bare feet. She slipped into the gown. There was one large window but, because it was dark outside, all Grace could see was blackness behind a white sheer curtain. There was an adjustable metal bed covered by a thin mattress in the middle of the room and a large lamp dangling overhead. Grace noticed a stack of linens—swaddling blankets and towels—on the chair next to the bed. The more Grace looked around, the more nervous she became. As she stood frozen behind the curtain she felt a wave of pain, like the worst menstrual cramp she'd ever had. It hurt so much, she let out a moan.

"Oh, that was just a contraction. Those help push the baby out. Your body is getting to work." The nurse washed her hands by the sink and continued getting the room ready, pulling the sheets down, turning on lamps. She grabbed an electric razor. "Lay down over there on the table. I need to shave your pubic hair."

Grace had never been so scared in her life. She stared at the razor, then at the bed.

"You heard me, we need to shave you down there." The nurse gave a hurried look and scooted Grace over to the bed.

Grace had heard whispers about what a contraction was from the other girls, but she wasn't sure how best to deal with them. The pain was like nothing she'd experienced before. Was she supposed to count to ten while breathing in? Or three counts to inhale, three counts to exhale? She tried distracting herself as the contractions came and went. She thought of Peter, and the first time they had met. She pictured his face across from her at the dinner table at Talbot House. But this only made her sad, angry even. After all, he'd put her in this position in the first place! But if he was dead, she couldn't feel anger toward him. The uncertainty made her desperate. So she tried instead to picture herself on a blanket in the backyard of her childhood home reading a book in the warm sun.

The contractions became more regular and came on stronger. Within an hour or so another nurse had joined them. She asked Grace, who was pacing around the room, to lie down on the bed so that she could check how much she had dilated. Grace couldn't keep her legs from shaking when the nurse went in with her fingers. She felt sick.

"Wow! 7 centimeters!" She turned to the other nurse. "How are the contractions?"

"One minute apart. Do you want me to go fetch the doctor?"

"Yes, I think you should. If Grace...It's Grace, right?" Grace nodded. "If Grace only came in here less than an hour ago and she's already dilated 7 centimeters, this could go pretty fast." The other nurse rushed off.

Grace's gaze focused first on the clock that hung on the wall above the door. 11:45 p.m. The baby could be born on June 6 or 7; it was up for grabs at this point. Grace thought she liked the sound of 6-6-1943. She couldn't help herself and had two names picked out: Nancy if it was a girl, Andrew if it was a boy. To the right of the clock was a framed print she recognized

from an art history course at Smith: Gustav Klimt's
'Portrait of Serena Lederer'. Serena, with her rosy
cheeks and beautiful white dress, seemed to peer directly at Grace, comforting her, telling her everything
was going to be alright.

The doctor arrived, wearing a long cotton smock.
A hood covered his head. Grace could only really see
his nose, as he also wore thickly framed glasses and a
mask.

"Hello, Grace. I'm Dr. Sullivan. How are we doing
here?" He washed his hands at the sink, then pulled
a stool on wheels up to the foot of the bed. "Go ahead
and place your feet in the stirrups here. Let's have a
look." The doctor pulled the lamp closer and adjusted
the light. "Ah yes, I can see the baby's head crowning."

Oh my God! Grace thought to herself, before another contraction rushed over her like a wave.

"It's okay, give into it, Grace. You're almost ready
to push." One of the nurses asked the doctor if he
wanted to administer twilight sleep, then turned on
the heat lamp and started laying out blankets.

"No. I think we're too far along now." He replied.
The other nurse stood by, handing the doctor various
instruments with one hand and a cloth with the other.
Grace grabbed hold of the metal frame on the bed,

scrunched up her face, and pressed her lips together hard.

"I have to poop!" The words flew out of Grace's mouth before she even knew what she was saying.

"That's normal Grace, that just means it's time to pu…" Before the doctor could even say the word, Grace found herself pushing with all her might. "That's it Grace, push, you're almost there."

Grace let out a sound she had never made before —"*Oooooohhhhh, arghhhhh!*"—as if she were a cave woman. And, just like that, she felt a huge sense of relief and heard a baby crying.

"It's a girl!" The doctor said sweetly, handing the baby to the nurse. "She'll get her cleaned up while I attend to the afterbirth."

"The afterbirth?" Grace wasn't sure whether she understood him correctly.

"Yes, your placenta. It's been growing in your uterus, nourishing your baby all this time. Don't worry. It won't take long. We just need to make sure it's all out." The doctor stretched his right arm alongside Grace's body, toward her abdomen, and pressed lightly. Grace felt a warm sensation as something large and red plopped out of her body. She quickly looked the other way. One of the nurses came over to Grace and placed a cool washcloth on her forehead. It was the kindest thing anyone had done for her so far.

"Don't I get to hold her?" Grace asked as she looked over to where the baby was being weighed and swaddled.

"No, I don't think that's a good idea. We don't want the babies to bond with their birth mothers. We'll just get her cleaned up. You're better off just letting us bring the baby to the nursery where she'll be picked up by her new family."

"So you already know who the parents will be?" Grace had been told there was a waitlist for the babies, but she didn't know her baby would be gone so quickly.

"Yes. Because this is a closed adoption, I can't share any information with you, but I can say that they are a very nice and loving couple."

"I would like to hold her, just for a moment, if that's okay. Please?" Feeling a sense of panic at the prospect of them carrying away her sweet baby, she looked over toward the other nurse with pleading eyes.

The nurse who had placed a washcloth on Grace's forehead went over to her colleague, who'd been keeping the crying baby warm under the lamp. Grace overheard them talking in hushed tones. The doctor continued to tend to Grace, as stitches were needed. Grace felt exhausted, yet relieved that the birth was over. She looked over at the clock—ten minutes past midnight. Her baby's birthday was June 7. She was two weeks early, but as far as Grace could tell, she was as healthy as could be. The baby had stopped crying, and the kinder of the two nurses brought her over to Grace. Although it hurt, she tried to sit up so she could hold her baby properly.

The world seemed to stop as the nurse deposited the precious bundle in Grace's arms. A warm, euphoric wave of wonder traveled through her as she looked down at her baby. She had dark hair, like Peter.

"I'll give you two a moment, but then we really need to take the baby away. I'm going to go make a telephone call, but I'll be back." The nurse left the room.

"My work here is done." Dr. Sullivan turned off the bright overhead light, pushed back the stool, and went to the sink to wash his hands. "You did a good job, Grace. The nurses will give you some medicine to help with the pain. For now, try to rest." Dr. Sullivan winked at her and closed the door behind him.

Grace found herself alone in the room at ten minutes past midnight, with her beautiful baby girl in her arms. She thought how surreal it was to have had this creature living inside her for the past nine months. The idea alone was too much to fathom. She leaned in closer to her baby's head, which smelled like peonies on the first day of summer. She had never smelled anything so lovely and sweet in her life.

"Hello, sweet girl. Welcome to the world." Grace felt a lump move through her throat and tried to swallow it. She marveled at how giant her index finger looked inside the grasp of her baby's tiny fist. "I'm Grace, your mama." She said as tears filled her eyes. "I'm so sorry that I can't take you with me. But I promise, it's for the best."

Even though she'd had nine months to think about it, Grace honestly hadn't anticipated how she would react in this moment. Giving birth, holding her baby for the first time—it had stolen the breath right out of her. She realized she'd been lying to herself all along, to protect herself. Up until the birth, she'd had herself convinced that this was a transaction. She would deliver the baby, and the baby would be given to parents who could better care for her. End of story. Grace would move on with her life. But now, here she was, this beautiful creature. An actual living, breathing human, with hair and tiny hands. Grace kissed her on the head and whispered words she'd never expected to whisper, words that just came out: "I love you."

The door swung open and the moment was over.

"Here, let me take her so you can get your rest." The nurse reached for the baby. Grace held her more tightly.

"No. Please, just a little while longer."

"Grace, come on. It's time."

"But what if her new parents turn out to be terrible people?"

"I assure you, they're very nice people. I'm not authorized to tell you anything more, but trust me, she'll be in good hands." Before Grace could say another word, the nurse carefully but firmly took the baby from her. "Come here little one, let's get you to the nursery and get you a bottle. The other nurse will be back in a second to attend to you, Grace."

When her baby was torn from her arms, Grace felt the same sense of abandonment she'd felt at thirteen, when her mother had left. She remembered hearing the back door slam and watching, in shock, as her mother got into a taxi cab. They had locked eyes for a moment, but her mother was quick to avert her gaze as the car drove off. Now Grace was the one who was doing the leaving. It was almost too much for her to bear as she sat in a metal bed, with tender, leaking breasts, wearing a diaper to absorb all the bleeding, her only companions a dark window and ticking clock. She felt like the world's greatest disappointment.

4
The White House Dinner

Wednesday, April 20, 1960

The latest gossip in town was that President Eisenhower's son, John, and his wife, Barbara, were throwing a fete at the White House for John's birthday. The president was away conducting trade talks. Only the family's closest friends from Gettysburg would be invited, along with their Washington pals. Grace couldn't believe her eyes when she opened her mailbox to find an ecru envelope with the official White House seal stamped in gold on the outside.

Major and Mrs. John S.D. Eisenhower
request the pleasure of the company of

*Mr. and Mrs. Ed Kingston at a dinner dance on
Monday, May 2, 1960, at eight o'clock
The White House*

Inside, there was a small card that said:

*Please send response to The Social Secretary, The
White House, at your earliest convenience.*

And then another even smaller card that simply read:

Black Tie

Now, that's classy! Three cards for one party, she thought.

Grace called Jane and then Lois, to ask what they
were wearing. They immediately began planning a
special trip to Philadelphia to find fashionable dresses
suitable for the occasion. In the City of Brotherly
Love, Grace chose a strapless number, with a tulle
skirt that had small silk roses sewn along the hem.
Three layers of organza—light pink, dark pink, and
green—swirled around her, emphasizing her hour-
glass figure. In order to stay *en vogue* with her friends,
which she secretly hated doing, she accented the dress
with the pearl necklace Ed had given her for their

tenth wedding anniversary. Lois and Jane went for a more sophisticated look, selecting black satin dresses that essentially looked the same. The only difference between their sartorial choices was their jewelry—pearls for Lois, diamonds for Jane.

Two weeks later, as the sweetness in the air ripened, turning spring into summer, the women insisted they all go down to Washington together, so that no one missed a thing. Jane and Jack arranged for the limousine, because Jack "knew a guy." Grace felt butterflies in her stomach and pinched herself. She couldn't believe that she was actually going to dinner at the White House. She, Grace Gilmartin! Who could imagine in a million years this night would happen?

Jane quickly reapplied her lipstick, then clicked her make-up mirror closed. Lois asked Grace whether she had anything stuck in her teeth. After the security guard peeked inside their limo and gave the driver a nod of approval, they pulled up the round driveway. Grace stepped out carefully, so as not to fall in her heels. She took a deep breath of the fresh night air—a relief, after enduring the smell of alcohol evaporating from people's pores inside the car. The city lights twinkled against the black sky, making the stars less visible than they had been in Gettysburg. Grace could still feel the warmth of the gin moving through her bloodstream, from the pre-party Jane and Jack had hosted in their hotel room, making her feel looser and less censored. The 80-mile drive from home was too far for a dinner and dance that started at 8:00 p.m. Reserving rooms at the Willard Hotel had been well worth the hefty price tag. This was a once-in-a-life-time event! Plus, no one was interested in yawning back up to Gettysburg once the festivities were over.

Grace smoothed out the skirt of her dress and fol-lowed the group into the White House entrance hall, where they lined up on a red carpet and began a slow march inside. As the women and their husbands ap-proached the main dining room, they saw a seating chart perched on an easel.

"Now, this is the defining moment." Jane blurted. "Who's sitting closest to the host? And who sits by the bathrooms?"

Though Grace didn't want to admit it to the group, she felt a slight pang of disappointment when she saw she was seated toward the back of the ballroom. But, she was in good company—that's where all the Gettys-burg guys and gals were.

Lois downplayed their lesser status—"Hey, I'm just happy to be here"—and walked into the ballroom, where a jazz quartet was playing. Lois grabbed Grace's hand. "Isn't this a dream?" she gushed. "Can you believe we're at the White House?"

"No, I can't." Grace peered around the room, taking it all in. The chandeliers, the rich, maroon plush carpet that framed the wooden dance floor, the floor-to-ceiling drapes—it was all so grand, so regal. The room smelled of lilies. At the front of the room, near the jazz band, she saw John and Barbara greeting people. Barbara looked stunning, in a floor length navy-blue gown. Her diamond necklace, with sapphires that matched her dress, cast a kaleidoscope of light on the ceiling above her. The Gettysburg crew of six stuck close together—there must have been at least fifty people besides them in the room, none of whom they knew.

"I'm kind of surprised Olga and Ethel weren't invited," Grace whispered into Lois' ear.

"I'm not. Their husbands don't golf, plus they're not *that* close with Barbara—just the occasional chit-chat, that sort of thing." Lois said, adjusted her gloves. "I'm actually relieved they weren't invited. The last thing we need is Ethel here, brown-nosing."

"I suppose you're right. Barbara can't invite everyone in town."

"We should probably say 'hello' to the hosts, don't you think?" Ed suggested to the group.

"That would be the appropriate protocol," Jack said agreeably, and they all made their way to the front. Jack was the first to extend his hand to John Eisenhower, patting him on the shoulder a little too hard with his left. "Mighty fine place you got here, John, almost as nice as the Gettysburg Country Club clubhouse." Jane rolled her eyes and gently shoved Jack aside.

"Don't mind Jack and his lame jokes, John. Thank you so much for inviting us. This is all so special. What a great way to celebrate your birthday." Jane reached out a white-gloved hand.

Grace complimented Barbara on her gown, while Ed asked John what the electricity bill was like for a place that big. A White House photographer approached the group. Lois practically knocked Grace over trying to stand next to Barbara. The camera's flash cast stars in their eyes and the moment was captured in time.

When the group finally arrived at their table, Ed pulled out Grace's chair for her, making sure she faced the Eisenhowers and had the best view, then he sat down across from her. Grace took in the room. There was a soft roar of boisterous laughter and clinking crystal. An army of wait staff paraded around with finesse, pouring wine into glasses before they were emptied. She looked at Ed and it occurred to her that he was uncomfortable. This scene was not his scene. He always coughed when he was feeling awkward, a tiny yet frequent *heh-hem* that drove Grace nuts. Ed had never been good at chit-chat. He could talk numbers any day of the week. Tell him about your bookkeeping, ask him any tax question—those things would make his eyes light up. But talk about politics, movies, literature, things Grace enjoyed discussing? Forget it. Although she'd chosen straight-arrow Ed as a partner because he made her feel safe, an underlying contempt for him had slowly formed over the years— like a callus. Looking at him here tonight, she realized that although safety and predictability went hand in hand, decades of experiencing it had left her with a thirst for adventure and excitement. The allure of the White House ballroom added fuel to this fire. Here she was, thirty-eight years old; it wouldn't be long before she was a dried up old prune. She thought what a shame it was not to have her mother as a benchmark, to see how she would age.

And that's when it happened. She looked up, and there he was. She had sworn she'd seen him last summer, too, on Labor Day weekend; a man in uniform accompanying Ike onto the golf course for the last tournament of the season. But she waved it away; it couldn't actually be *him*. After all, he was dead! Everyone has a doppelganger somewhere, right? But here he was again. She was so startled by the sight that she dropped her knife.

"Grace, are you okay? You look white as a sheet." Ed picked up her knife from the floor. "Grace?"

"What? Oh, yes. . .Yes, I'm fine. I thought I saw someone I knew, that's all. But, I think I'm mistaken." Despite her attempt to play it cool, her heart was racing. The tall, handsome man standing by the door with a headset on, speaking quietly into his sleeve, was definitely him. Peter. She was sure of it. His jet-black hair, his dark, friendly eyes, thick eyebrows, and—the feature that was truly indisputable—the mole on his left cheek. His posture was as she remembered it. He stood straight as a board, making his 6-foot-4-inch frame appear even more impressive. His broad shoulders were like the strong foundation of a building. He did a security sweep around the room with his eyes, and paused when his gaze reached Grace. She quickly reached for her napkin and placed it on her lap. She could still feel his eyes on her as she ran her fingers over the silverware.

Barbara began tapping a champagne glass with her knife and the band stopped playing. Grace's reverie ended. All eyes were trained toward the front of the room, but Grace's were fixed on Peter in the corner. She watched him watching her.

"Good evening, friends! Welcome! John and I are thrilled to have you here at the White House this evening. We had a chance to speak with most of you, but for those we haven't chatted to yet, please do stop by at some point this evening. Dinner is about to be served, followed by dancing. Also, we have a surprise guest appearance this evening." The room immediately exploded into soft speculative whispers. Barbara had to tap her glass again to call for quiet. "You'll see, all in good time. But first, a toast to all of you, our dear friends here tonight! Thank you for coming! And most importantly, happy birthday to my dear husband, John!" She raised her glass and everyone in the room followed suit and took a sip of their champagne. The band began to play again. Soft jazz music filled the air as the chatter resumed.

Jane held up her menu. "My stomach is growling just looking at this. Melba toast with cream of almond soup, roast stuffed pheasant with currant jelly and gravy, a tossed green salad with ranch dressing, and a bisque tart with brandied marron sauce! Must be nice to have a chef cook up these amazing things every night. How about it, Jack?"

"Must be nice for men at this table who have wives who cook for them at home," Jack barked, keeping his eyes on the menu in front of him. "Mine works in a diner, for Christ's sake, but she can't seem to make me more than a piece of toast."

"Let's keep it pleasant, shall we?" Lois interjected. "And what you say isn't true, Jack. Do you really think I have time to cook while running a newspaper?"

Before the first course arrived, Grace excused herself to visit the ladies' room. Peter was still standing by the door. Her legs were shaking as she stood up and her heart felt as though it was liable to burst out of her chest. She could feel her face becoming increasingly red as she made her way to the double doors that led out to the hallway. She didn't want to cause a scene, so she looked down as she pushed her way through the doors.

She felt a hand on her arm.

"Grace? I thought it was you." Grace brushed Peter's hand away gently.

"Not here," Grace whispered, looking his way but without eye contact. "Come out to the hallway in two minutes." Peter gave her a nod.

Grace ran to the bathroom, relieved to be alone and able to gather her thoughts. She walked up to the mirror, leaned on the sink, and stared at her reflection. "Come on Grace, get it together." She said under her breath. She saw the 20-year-old Smith College girl in front of her, only now with smile lines and a hint of crow's feet by her eyes. She took a few deep breaths to calm her nerves. But that didn't help. She began gasping for air and felt sweat beading on her forehead. She reached over for a hand towel, ran it under cold water, and dabbed at her head and neck. When that didn't help, she tried leaning forward, resting her elbows on her knees. It was as if all the emotions, all the shame she had buried deep inside all those years ago, had been released and were being burned up, like the sun's rays burning blades of grass through a magnifying glass. Her heart was a fiery blade of grass. What would she say to him after all these years? All this time she had thought he was dead, having never heard anything about him since that letter from Nancy. After giving up their baby, she had decided it was best to get on with her life and embarked on the fast track to graduate school. As a means of self preservation, she had erased everything that had happened and embraced a clean slate.

Slowly, Grace managed to regain control of her breath. She took a sip of water from the sink and wiped the palms of her hands across her hair, smoothing it out. Standing up tall, shoulders back, she walked out into the hallway. Peter was standing there, calm, collected, eyes so warm and deep she could've melted right into them.

"Grace, I..."

"I can't believe you're here, that it's you." She walked closer to him. She could smell his cologne: bergamot and musk. They stood there looking at each other, smiling, taking each other in as if studying a map. They both reached out at the same time and hugged each other.

"I wrote to you, you know? But there were no letters in return. I thought you were...dead!"

"What? You did? Grace, I'm so sorry! No, I didn't know. I was drafted four months before graduating. Any mail coming to Amherst was probably returned." Peter paused for a moment, swallowing a lump in his throat. "Grace, I thought of you each and every day. My biggest regret is not telling you that I loved you."

Grace did all she could to keep the tears from welling in her eyes, but failed. Peter took a handkerchief from his pocket and dabbed her cheek. She let him.

She wanted to tell him that, even though she had tried to forget and move on with her life, she couldn't. She wanted to tell him that she still kept a journal, because if she didn't write down her feelings her pain would eat her up from the inside. But she didn't.

"Why didn't you come find me at Smith? Or write to me? You knew I was there for another year."

"I know, Grace. I'm so sorry. With the war, I kept getting promoted and moved on to the next location. I barely had time to write to my parents. One year turned into two, then five. I figured you had probably moved on. I didn't want to burden you. Where do you live now?"

"Gettysburg. I'm a professor at the college there. I'm up for tenure this year." She sniffed, trying to regain composure.

"You're kidding! That's wonderful, Grace! Just what you always wanted! But what are the chances? I'm the President's Secret Service agent and always accompany him on the farm when he's there."

"So that *was* you last year out on the golf course during Labor Day weekend. I could have sworn I saw you. I thought I was going crazy!"

"Yes, I was there that weekend. I wish I'd known you were, too."

"So, you're a Secret Service agent? I thought you wanted to go into the FBI!"

"Well, don't you think this is a close second?" Peter said, laughing. Grace laughed, too, which felt good. "I see you're still wearing the watch I gave you."

Jane pushed through the double doors.

"Grace? We're waiting for you to start the first course."

Grace jumped at the sound of her friend's voice. She felt like a thief caught in the act, even though there wasn't anything particularly suspicious going on.

"So sorry, Jane! I'll be right there." Jane furrowed her eyebrows, then disappeared back into the ballroom.

"I have to see you again," Peter said as he reached for her hands. "We have so much to catch up on. I have so many questions for you."

"Well, you know where to find me. I really must go, before they send a search party." Grace handed Peter his handkerchief.

"Keep it, please." At that moment the walkie-talkie clipped to Peter's belt chirped. "I have to go, too." He spoke some sort of code language into the device, winked at Grace, and walked down the hallway.

As Grace sat back down at the dinner table, everyone was grabbing for their soup spoons.

"Where have you been?" Ed asked. "We've been waiting for you."

"I'm so sorry. There was a line for the bathroom. I think someone may have gotten sick." Grace was surprised by how quickly she could concoct a fib and how believable it sounded.

"Okay, well, the food is getting cold." Ed started slurping his soup.

The courses kept coming and the wine kept flowing, but Grace could not get her mind off Peter, no matter how hard she tried. No one at the table seemed to notice, as Jane and Lois continued commenting on every single dress in the room and Robert, Jack, and Ed took inventory of the men's watch brands. Grace had consumed at least four drinks by 10:00. Two was usually her max, but tonight a sudden *laissez faire* attitude took over here. Seeing Peter standing in the corner again, she longed to excuse herself from the table. But that would be too obvious. As dessert plates were cleared, cognac was poured, and cigarettes lit. The jazz quartet continued to play just loud enough for people to have to raise their voices to speak to their neighbors.

Barbara Eisenhower tapped her glass once again. "Okay everybody, I'd like to announce our special guests tonight."

"I knew it! Good ol' Ike made time for us after all!" Jack clapped his hands and rubbed them together.

"Don't get your hopes up, sweetie. Mr. President is off on a diplomatic tour of Asia. I read it in the good ol' *Gettysburg Times* this morning." Jane swirled her cognac, watching its thick legs run down the sides of her glass. "Isn't that right, Lois?"

"That's correct. Which reminds me, we must get our hands on that photo they took of us tonight for the paper! This will be front page news. Okay, shhh! Barbara is about to say who it is…"

"Ladies and gentlemen, it's my pleasure to present to you…The Everly Brothers!"

The crowd went wild. Chairs were pushed back, drinks spilled, and people ran to the dance floor as the duo took the stage and started singing 'Wake up Little Susie'. Jane and Lois clapped their hands and swayed their hips, right into the next song, and the next… During the fourth number, Grace appeared on the dance floor.

"Where have you been all this time, Grace? You're missing it!" Jane grabbed her hands and started swirling her around.

"I wasn't feeling so well. I think I had too much to drink."

"Oh honey, you never could handle too much alcohol. Want me to come sit down with you?"

"No, that's okay. I see Ed is at our table. I'll go sit with him for a bit."

And she did, for a while. When the Everly Brothers announced their last song for the night—'All I Have to Do is Dream'—Ed asked Grace to dance. As she felt Ed's hands on her waist and his hot breath against her ear, her eyes were fixed the entire time on the Secret Service officer in the corner. And his eyes on hers.

5

English 101

Friday, May 13, 1960

Locals would say how all roads lead to Gettysburg. For Grace and Ed, this had definitely been the case. Grace and Ed moved to Gettysburg when Grace got her job teaching a decade ago at Gettysburg College. Like the train in *The Little Engine that Could*, Grace had chugged along steadily over the years, slowly climbing the academic mountain. It wasn't easy. People around her would say things like "Graduate school? Why put yourself through all that aggravation when you're going to get married and have a family?" People thought graduate school was a waste of time for women, seeing as the husband was always assumed to be the breadwinner. She was living in a world where women became nurses, not doctors. Kindergarten teachers, not professors.

But that didn't stop Grace. She wanted to improve her chances in the job market. She had written her dissertation on the works of her favorite author, Ayn Rand. And, after applying to various teaching positions along the East Coast and receiving rejection letter after rejection letter, she had finally landed an assistant professor position at Gettysburg College. Though female professors were still vastly outnumbered, there were two other women teaching in the English Department. She and Ed had been elated at the prospect of moving to a small, sweet college town. After experiencing so many losses, it finally felt like Grace was on track, and making gains. The gold watch on her wrist, the one Peter gave her the last night they were together at Smith, was the only thing linking her to the darkest secret of her past.

Grace didn't like keeping things from her husband, but she felt she had no other choice. What was the point in upsetting him? The prospect of Ed ever finding out about Peter, and the baby she gave away, did scare her, though. Hanging onto such big secrets was debilitating. She was tempted on occasion to ask her doctor to write a prescription for the "nerve pills" her mother used to take. But Grace didn't want to end up like her mother, so instead she poured herself into her career. Literature had been her savior growing up. Now, guiding her students through her favorite books was saving her as an adult. She loved teaching; it allowed her to share her knowledge with young people, and to continue learning herself. Being in an academic environment and spending her days on campus—talking with her colleagues about their research at lunch in the dining hall, and having access to the extensive collections in the college library—made Grace content. She felt safe in her bubble. She had found her place in the world. Most of all, she loved her students, especially those with a desire to take their studies further, as she had.

Mary was an exceptional student. She was bright enough to audit Grace's English 101 class as a 17-year-old high school senior. Under special circumstances, seniors at the local high school were permitted to earn college credit before enrolling in a university. College tuition cost $245 a year, and Mary wasn't sure how she was going to afford to attend full time after graduation on the pittance she made as a lifeguard at the country club. To help her save up some money, Grace had hired her on as her teaching assistant. Grace wasn't sure who was getting the better deal though. Mary helped her conduct research for scholarly articles and assemble her tenure portfolio, as well as other mundane administrative tasks, like making sure there was always paper on hand for the typewriter. This gave Grace the time and space she needed to work toward her own goals.

Today, Mary was reorganizing Grace's filing cabinet while Grace graded the personal essays she'd asked her students to write. She'd promised them that they would have their papers in hand after their final class, which was due to start in an hour. She pulled out the last one, Mary's—typically the easiest to grade—and set to work. As Grace read Mary's words, her eyes widened.

I've always struggled for a sense of belonging. When I was ten, we moved to Gettysburg for my father's job. That's around the same time that my parents told me I was adopted. They were unable to have children, and named me Mary after the Virgin Mary, because they felt so blessed.

Grace looked up from the paper and watched Mary shuffling through some folders. Grace couldn't help but fantasize that this young woman, her bright student who loved literature as much as she did, was in fact her daughter. Age-wise it made sense. But what were the odds? Grace resumed reading Mary's essay with increasing interest. There were physical similarities between them—brown eyes and high cheekbones—and Grace couldn't help but study Mary's posture and hands as she moved about the room. Mary must have felt Grace's eyes on her, as she stopped and turned around.

"Is everything all right, professor?" Mary asked with a nervous laugh.

"Oh, my goodness, yes! I'm sorry. I was just in the middle of reading your personal essay." Grace had been caught. Her face flushed.

"Oh, yes. I really enjoyed that assignment. I don't talk about the fact that I'm adopted with most people, so it was nice to be able to write about it. I feel like I can say so much more on paper than out loud."

"I know what you mean, Mary. I know what you mean." Grace shifted her weight in her chair. "Have you ever tried to find your birth mother?"

"No, it was a closed adoption. I consider my adoptive parents my true parents, and I know the woman who gave me up had good reason to do so. I'm not resentful or anything," Mary said thoughtfully. "But sometimes I wonder who she is, whether she's still alive, what she looks like...that sort of thing." Mary closed the filing cabinet.

"Yes. Well, I'm sure wherever she is, whoever she is, she would be proud to see what an intelligent young woman you've become." Grace swallowed hard. "You know, it feels a bit strange to be grading your paper while you're here in the room with me. Why don't you get some fresh air before class and I'll wrap up here?"

"Are you sure? I haven't completed my tasks and I'm really counting on the pay for the full hour."

"Yes, go ahead and take a walk. It's gorgeous outside. And don't worry about the pay; I've got you covered. I'll see you in class in a bit."

"Okay, great! Thank you, Professor Gilmartin." Mary grabbed her rucksack. "See you in class."

Grace continued to devour Mary's essay. But when she read that her parents had come from Colorado, she knew the chances that Mary was her long lost daughter were slim to none. She looked down at her nails. She hadn't realized she'd been gnawing away at them as she read. How could she be so stupid? Wishful thinking had gotten the better of her and now she felt ashamed. She took a deep breath, grabbed her grading pen, and gave Mary's essay an A+.

As the semester wound down for Grace's English 101 class, a buzz of excitement was in the air. Students were anxious about taking their exams, handing in their final papers, and heading off to their summer jobs. Grace absolutely loved teaching her students.

They kept her on her toes, and made her feel young with all their talk about Elvis Presley and the latest fads—A-line dresses and hiked-up hemlines—and the way they used the latest slang, like "Daddy-o" and "burn rubber."

Grace walked into her classroom on the third floor of Glatfelter Hall. A light breeze freshened the air as she laid the pile of personal essays on her desk. She never wrote grades on the cover page, so that students could note her comments first before finding their grade at the back. As it was the last class of the semester, today she would hold their papers hostage, to ensure they paid attention to her final lecture, before passing them out at the end.

While students streamed into the classroom, giggling, whispering, and playfully shoving each other, Grace prepared for the day's lesson, writing in big letters across the chalkboard—*Illicit vs. Forbidden Love*. The room grew increasingly quiet as the students took their seats. Grace put the chalk down and turned to face the class.

"Good morning, everyone."

"Good morning, Professor Gilmartin," the students replied in unison.

"I hope your final papers are going well. I've

marked your personal essays, which, along with the rest of your papers this semester, account for thirty percent of your grade. I'll hand them out at the end of class. Your final papers account for fifty percent and class participation for twenty, so today is your chance to shine one last time." Grace smiled as she looked around the room. "If you have any questions or concerns, you can come talk to me during office hours. This will be the last lecture of our overriding theme this semester: love in literature." Grace pointed to the chalkboard. She heard a nervous cough and the rustling of papers. Grace stood up, placed her hands on the desk in front of her and leaned toward the class.

"So today, we're talking about illicit versus forbidden love. It's important to know the difference. Illicit love is a sexual relationship outside of marriage, whereas forbidden love might refer to a romantic relationship between two individuals that is highly discouraged or strongly opposed by a third party, such as parents, or the public, for cultural, societal, political, or religious reasons. Both forms of love can be found in several of the novels and plays that we've discussed in class this term. Who can name a few? Peggy?"

"*Romeo and Juliet*?...As an example of forbidden love?"

"Yes. Anyone else?" Grace scanned the room.

"*Lady Chatterley's Lover*," offered Harry, one of the brightest students in the class. "It has both illicit and forbidden forms of love, because it's about a relationship outside of marriage that also crosses the line between the upper and lower classes."

"Yes, that's an excellent example. Anyone else?"

"*Tristan and Isolde*," Mary chimed in from the back row.

"Yes, one of my favorite forbidden love stories. Now, what do all of these stories of illicit and forbidden love have in common?"

James' hand shot up. "They're all stacked in a pile next to my mother's bed."

The classroom erupted in laughter.

"Good one, James. Glad to hear your mother is such an avid reader. Anyone else?"

Mary raised her hand. "They all have a tragic ending."

"Most do, yes, and why do you think that is? Why can't stories of illicit and forbidden love end happily ever after?" Grace found herself staring at the large maple tree just outside her window and her mind drifted to Peter. She could not seem to erase his face from her mind. His warm smile kept flashing through her head, like a moving picture.

"Professor Gilmartin?" James had his hand up again.

Grace jumped. "Oh, yes. My apologies. James, do you have an answer for us?"

"Stories about illicit and forbidden love can't end happily ever after because they weren't meant to be from the very beginning," James explained. "Someone always ends up getting hurt, which makes the stories tragic."

"That's right James. Tragic." Grace took a deep breath. She continued the lecture, then broke the students into pairs to discuss their favorite books featuring illicit or forbidden love—or both. When the class was almost over Grace said, "Okay, time to wrap up. Don't forget to put your final papers in my mailbox by the end of next week, if you haven't already. You'll receive your grade by mail within the next few weeks. If you're taking English 200 with me in the fall, I've posted your assigned reading for the summer here on the chalkboard. Consider it good beach reading."

After class, Grace headed to the college mail room where she found a pile of students' final papers in her cubby hole, as well as a large envelope with her name on the front along with a stamp that read, "Strictly Confidential." She'd never received an envelope like this before, but she wasn't particularly concerned—she was on her way home and could open it there rather than in front of Trudy the secretary, who was always poking around in Grace's business. Trudy looked up from her typewriter.

"Have a good afternoon, Professor Gilmartin—and a good summer, for that matter!"

"You too, Trudy. I'll be back at some point to mail off my students' final papers, but if I don't see you, have a wonderful summer."

Grace's high heels clicked as she left the English Department mailroom, took the stairs, and walked through the front door into the sunshine. She lived just two blocks from Glatfelter Hall, in a beautiful Cape Cod style home on West Broadway. Walking across the serene campus, she remembered Ed had a tennis match after work and that he would be home late for dinner. Maybe she could tackle one of those final papers tonight.

Since the White House dinner, Grace had tried everything she could to stay busy and keep her mind occupied. But it was no use. She couldn't stop thinking about Peter. What were the odds of seeing him again? The first time, last Labor Day weekend at the country club, she had convinced herself that her eyes had been playing tricks on her. But at the White House dinner there he was, right in front of her, after all these years. A car honked and she froze in the middle of the street. She was so lost in thought, she'd carelessly crossed Lincoln Avenue without looking left or right. Raising her hand in embarrassment, she continued walking the final block home.

She and Ed had found the house together ten years ago, when she'd finally landed her job at the college. She was twenty-eight and had just finished graduate school. Most of her friends were already done having children by that point. Knowing kids were not on the cards for them, Ed had quietly removed the swing set from their large backyard. Grace, in turn, busied herself with converting one of their spare bedrooms into a guest room and the other into a home office. Despite the absence of children playing in their own backyard, their street was filled with kids playing kick the can in the median and racing around on their bikes. Grace had convinced herself that it was enough to hear other peoples' children shouting and having fun. After all, she had her cat, Shakespeare, a beautiful Persian who cuddled up on her lap every chance he could get.

"Well, hello there, Shakespeare." Grace unlocked the door and tossed her briefcase on a chair in the corner. She picked him up and held him close, caressing his soft fur. "Can you keep a secret, my friend?" She put the cat back down on the ground and he rubbed against her ankles. "Oh right, food first." Grace bent down and filled Shakespeare's bowl.

As she stood up, she caught a glimpse of her wedding photo on the kitchen wall. She looked deep into Ed's face and her own. Ed looked every bit himself—self-assured and proud, as though he had just won a prize at the county fair. Had *she* truly been happy that day? She had always thought so, but now she noticed a distance in her eye. Seeing Peter all these years later, she wondered if it was possible to love two men. Her love for Ed was a carefully constructed piece of classical music, while her love for Peter was more like jazz, driven by passion and unpredictability. The theme of the class she'd just taught felt too close to home. Her love for Peter was solidly in the "illicit" category; she was a married woman. If she was honest though, she very much hoped to see him again.

Grace dug her confidential post out of her briefcase. She ripped it open to find a letter from the English Department stating that her application for tenure was under review. A final decision would be made before the commencement of the new academic year, in mid-August. Grace read the letter four more times. She was almost there, her dream had almost reached fruition. Teaching English Literature as a tenured college professor would mean she had the security she had craved her entire life, that she would be able to keep doing what she loved until she decided to retire. Grace jumped up and down and danced around the kitchen. Shakespeare scampered across the room.

As Grace laid the letter on the kitchen counter, the doorbell rang. The silhouetted figure on the other side of her sheer curtains was not familiar. She opened the door.

"Peter!"

"Hello, Grace." Dimples appeared as he handed Grace a bouquet of pink and white peonies.

"How on earth did you find me?"

"Well, I *am* a Secret Service agent, you know." Peter winked. Grace stood there in shock. After a moment of silence, Peter asked, "Can I come in?"

Grace peered onto the street, looking left and right, making sure none of her neighbors were watching. She knew how small town gossip starts. "Yes, of course, come in! I'm sorry, where are my manners? Can I get you anything to drink?" Grace led him to the screened-in porch at the back of the house.

"Anything cold will do."

"Iced tea?"

"Perfect."

"Go ahead and sit down. I'll be right back." Grace scurried around the kitchen, her hands shaking as she looked for a vase in the cupboards. Flustered, she stuck the flowers in a highball glass and filled it with water, then grabbed two more glasses for the iced tea. She glanced at her reflection in a mirror hanging by the sink. Her hair was all over the place after her tenure letter celebration boogie. She tried tucking strands behind her ears and smoothed out what she could. After a few deep breaths, she joined Peter on the white wicker loveseat. "I'm sorry, I must look like a mess," Grace said as she put the tray down on the table. "I just arrived home from teaching my last class for the semester."

"Grace Gilmartin, a professor! That was always your dream."

"You remember that?" Grace blushed as she poured their iced tea.

"Of course! I always loved that you were such a go-getter. So driven, determined to get what you want."

"Well, I suppose I had to fight for it, yes. Things

don't come to women as easily as they do to men, you know." Grace smiled.

"That's true, I suppose. *La vie n'est pas juste.*"

When Grace looked confused, Peter asked "Didn't you study abroad to learn French? In Quebec? Because Paris wasn't an option due to the war?"

"Ah, but that was a long time ago."

Peter leaned in closer. He still smelled like sandalwood and soap. "Grace, I thought you were the most extraordinary young woman I'd ever met." A lock of dark hair curled at his brow. He looked exactly the same as when she'd first met him, except for a dash of gray around his temples. Grace saw the top button of his blue shirt was undone. Her hands were shaking as she sipped her iced tea. Shakespeare jumped up on Peter's lap.

"Hello, there." Peter stroked Shakespeare's fur, making him purr. Peter glanced around the room, turning to look out the window at the manicured backyard. "Looks like you've carved out a nice life for yourself here, Grace. I'm really happy for you."

"What about you? Are you married? Have any kids?" Grace noticed the absence of a wedding band on his finger.

"No, and no. After college I drove ambulances

in North Africa, in Operation Torch, under Commander Eisenhower. I saw a lot of my buddies die in front of my eyes. I had a couple of close calls myself. It all helped me realize how much I wanted to continue to serve and protect people. Ike asked me to be one of his guards. I was there with him in Normandy, on D-Day, and I've been with him ever since. A wife and kids don't really fit into the picture, I guess."

"I can't even imagine what you've seen and been through!" Grace said as she raised her glass to her mouth. "But what you have now seems exactly what you always wanted."

"It sounds like we both got what we wanted, professionally at least." Peter looked down at his shoes. "Grace, I couldn't believe my eyes when I saw you at the White House dinner. I mean, you're the only woman who has ever really meant anything to me."

Grace gasped, accidentally spitting a small ice cube back into her glass. She wanted to tell him that she felt the same way. She wanted to tell him that somewhere in the world there was a 17-year-old walking around as a result of their love. All these years she'd kept Peter and the maternity home a secret from everyone, except Nancy. Keeping everything bottled up inside was killing her, so she did her best to compartmentalize.

But she knew she was walking a dangerous line, for herself and for those around her.

What time was it? Only 4:00 p.m. Ed wouldn't be home for at least another three hours.

Peter reached over and took her hand. The cat jumped off his lap. "Look, Grace, I'm not here to disrupt your life. It's just, when I saw you at the White House and found out that you live in Gettysburg, I knew I had to see you again."

"I know. It's crazy when you think about it. What are the odds?" Grace crossed her legs toward Peter.

"As I'm sure you're already aware, President Eisenhower is retiring here when his second term ends. I'll be stationed here for at least another year."

Grace cleared her throat. "Wow, a whole year. That's a good chunk of time!"

"The State of Pennsylvania is going to fill the president's security void by providing executive protection after he retires. I'll be part of Ike's protective detail, along with two state troopers. We'll take turns spending the night at the farm, providing round-the-clock surveillance. After all, Eisenhower does have access to the highest level state secrets and nuclear codes."

"I did read something about that in the paper, come to think of it." Grace wondered how she would deal with the temptation of knowing Peter would be living mere miles away for an entire year.

Peter stood up abruptly. "I'd better be going. I'm sure your husband will be home soon. And your children will probably be home from school?"

"Peter..." Grace grabbed his hand. It felt warm and rough against hers. "Don't go. Please, stay. My husband Ed won't be home until later. I don't have kids. Well, I..." She was about to tell him. Now seemed like the right moment.

"Okay, I suppose I could stay a bit longer." Peter sat back down and leaned back. Grace pulled a roll of peppermints from her skirt pocket.

"Would you like one?"

"Sure." Peter popped a peppermint into his mouth and sneezed three times, making Shakespeare jump. Grace burst out laughing.

"What's so funny?" Peter asked, raising his eyebrows in confusion.

"I just remembered that you always sneeze three times when you have peppermint and..."

"Red wine!" they said in unison, chuckling.

Their laughter trailed off and they sat in silence, caught in each other's eyes. Peter reached for Grace's hands. She felt nineteen again. They were kissing, soft at first, then ravenously, like two people starved for food. Before Grace knew it, she was unbuttoning his shirt and kicking off her heels.

"Come upstairs." Grace led the way, not wanting to waste a moment. It was too wrong for them to make love on the bed she shared with Ed, so she pulled Peter into the guest room. On the quilted mattress they went at it like teenagers, blood racing through their veins. She and Ed had never made love like this. When it was over, they lay in each other's arms, breathing heavily, laughing and basking in each other's warmth. Grace turned to Peter.

"Wow!"

"Wow is right. Jesus, Grace! That was incredible. Do you mind if I have a smoke?" Peter tenderly wiped a lipstick smudge from Grace's cheek with his thumb.

"No, of course not. Wait. I have a pack in the other room. I could do with one, too." Grace rose and quickly retrieved the pack and an ashtray from her bedroom. They lit up together and lay there, looking up at the ceiling, laughing and reminiscing about their college years.

Peter exhaled a big puff of smoke. "You want to know my biggest regret?"

"What? Tell me." Grace snuggled up onto his chest. She could hear his heartbeat.

"That I lost track of you. I mean, there was a world war, yes, and you went off to Quebec, but…"

"Peter, I didn't go to Quebec." Grace's voice was flat.

A car door slammed.

"Shit! What time is it? That's Ed! What's he doing home so soon?" Grace jumped off the guest bed and threw on her clothes, tearing her stocking in the process. There was no time to worry about details.

"Quick, Peter! You have to get out of here! Use the front door. Ed parks in the back."

"Okay, okay. But Grace, I need to see you again. There's so much we need to talk about. I can't leave you like this." Peter pulled up his pants and buttoned his shirt.

"I know. I know." She said, nudging him gently toward the stairs. "But you have to get out of here, *now*!" Grace followed him down the steps and gave Peter a push out the door. She saw Lois drive by. "Oh my God! Peter, duck!" Peter followed her command. She waited for the coast to clear. "Okay, go!" She took a deep breath. He turned, looked her straight in the eyes, and kissed her. His breath smelled of cigarettes and peppermint.

"Goodbye, Grace. You know where to find me. Probably better than me coming here again."

"Yes. Goodbye, Peter. Quick, go!" Grace closed the door softly, then rushed into the kitchen just as Ed flung open the back door, walked in, and tossed his keys on the countertop.

"Grace, I'm home!" He bellowed, without looking up, setting his briefcase down.

"I'm right here. And you're home early. I thought you had a tennis tournament." Grace replied, smoothing out her hair while pouring a glass of water. She turned to him with a smile.

"Yeah, one of the guys pulled a muscle, so we had to reschedule. What's for dinner?" Ed laid down the *Gettysburg Times* and scanned the room.

"I was going to heat up the meatloaf we had last night. Sorry, Ed. I didn't have time to give it any more thought. I could whip up some mashed potatoes to go with it if you'd like. How does that sound?"

"Who are those flowers from? And why is there a big hole in your stockings?"

Grace's pulse raced and her face grew flushed. "Oh, no! I didn't notice the tear." Grace reached down and stuck her finger in the hole. "It must have been Shakespeare. Those flowers are from Trudy, the secretary, a sort of end-of-semester gift." Grace's lie kept growing. "And, because I received a letter from the department saying that I'm up for tenure this fall…"

"Grace, that's amazing! Congratulations! Just what you've always hoped for. Come here!" Ed held out his arms wide and Grace walked over, allowing him to enfold her in his arms. He kissed the top of her head. "Let me take you out for dinner to celebrate!"

"Oh, Ed, you don't have to do that. I'm perfectly fine staying here. Plus we haven't budgeted for it."

"No, come on. You deserve it. Why don't you put on that green dress I love? I'll call the Peace Light Inn and make a reservation."

Grace wasn't really in the mood. She felt like an electric current was running through her veins. Although she would have rather stayed home to contemplate what had just happened, she didn't want to blow her cover and decided to relent. After all, Ed usually kept a tight watch on their spending and was not one to splurge on dinners out. She would hate to spoil his generous gesture.

Grace ran upstairs and took a quick shower; she could still smell Peter on her skin. She put on her green sheath dress and dark-pink kitten heels and tiptoed into the guest room to smooth out the bedspread and clear the ashtray of evidence. She gazed at herself in the vanity mirror while brushing her hair and felt younger, lighter, sexier. It was as though a long-lost inner flame had been reignited; she seemed to glow. The sensation reminded her of the feeling she had had when Mrs. Hamilton had suggested the prospect of college all those years ago—a new door opening onto wonderful opportunities.

They drove to the Peace Light Inn and were seated by the front window, overlooking the battlefield and the Eternal Light Peace Memorial, which had been dedicated in 1938 by FDR himself. Ed ordered a Manhattan for himself and a vodka Martini with extra olives for Grace.

"A toast to Professor Grace Gilmartin, the smartest, most beautiful woman I know, who is officially up for tenure. Cheers!" Ed raised his glass and nodded toward Grace.

"Aww...thank you, Ed. Cheers!" Grace clinked her glass against his and took a big swig, almost finishing half of it in one go.

"Whoa, Grace! Go easy."

"I've had a busy day. Teaching really is a lot of work. I'm going to miss it this summer, though. It always feels like such a long stretch until the fall semester starts up again."

The waitress stopped by to take their order. Grace knew what Ed would choose the moment she laid eyes on the menu. Steak, medium, and a baked potato with sour cream and chives. He was a creature of habit. Everything was predictable. This made life with him easy, or boring, depending on how you looked at it. Always the same blue button-down shirt. Always the same thing for breakfast—two eggs over easy with rye toast, like her father. Always the same coffee mug, newspaper, and brand of cigarettes. Grace had initially loved this about him: his stability, his familiarity, his steadiness. Maybe it was because she didn't want to find herself abandoned again, but she had never liked surprises, at least, not after her mother left. With Ed, she'd always felt a deep sense of loyalty and simplicity. She'd felt safe.

Ed excused himself to use the restroom. Grace stared out the window, feeling guilty. Here her husband was, treating her so well when she had just slept with another man—in their own home! Ed was such a devoted husband; he would never dream of doing anything to hurt her. Her napkin was folded neatly on her lap. The salt and pepper shakers stood next to each other on the table like a bride and groom at the altar. She felt a sudden jolt of paranoia, as though the people at the table next to her might smell the sex on her and start chanting "cheater!", "whore!"

But she couldn't deny that something had shifted inside of her. This was the first time she'd felt alive in years. She wanted, needed, *craved* more of Peter. He was her new bad habit. But all bad habits have consequences; she knew this. She'd witnessed her parents' marriage fail. Did what had happened earlier that afternoon mean her own marriage was doomed as well? Then her thoughts turned to all she stood to lose besides Ed. Her job and reputation were sacred to her. And she loved her adopted hometown.

Ed returned from the restroom and sat down. He stared out the window with Grace for a moment and then said, out of the blue, "Hey, remember when we first met?"

"Yes—on the New York City Subway, of all places." Grace took a sip of her Martini. "You found me in a sea of people." She thought back to that time and how she had been offered a spot at the University of Pennsylvania but had chosen Columbia instead. If she was honest, she would admit that her decision was probably inspired by all the glamorous stories her mother used to tell her about "the city" when she was a child. Her mother had trained as a professional dancer in New York before she met Grace's father, who had seen her in a show and waited at the stage door to meet her. His charm eventually won her over. After all, he was a trained salesman, so much so that he had convinced her to give up her career and settle down with him in Massachusetts on a promise that she would be the queen of her suburban castle—and would want for nothing. After a couple of years she was wanting bad for her nerve pills. She would ask Grace to fetch them from her purse, which always hung from the doorknob in her bedroom.

Grace had met Ed under far less romantic circumstances. She'd been late to class one day and was digging in her pockets next to the subway entrance when Ed saw her token fall out. He retrieved it and used the opportunity to ask her for her phone number. Because she was in a rush, as well as thankful, she gave it to him. She rebuffed his advances for weeks, until she finally said "yes" to dinner, seeing it as a kind way to thank him.

Grace's mother had once told her that a big part of marriage is timing and circumstance—who you happen to cross paths with, and when. Had Grace not lost her subway token, she would most likely never have met Ed. She was so focused on her studies, she never really had the time or inclination to date. And the heartbreak she felt after losing her first love, then their child, had built a wall around her heart. Fellow graduate students referred to Grace as the "Ice Queen," due to her reluctance to share anything personal about herself or her past. It was true. Grace wasn't one to share much information. She was done with loss and was determined not to get distracted by love again. Her career would be her driving force.

But Ed had been persistent, teasing her out of her shell bit by bit. The more time they spent together, the more she enjoyed his company. Ed respected her. He listened patiently as she read him her dissertation and asked thoughtful questions. They had a few things in common: a love for tennis, the beach, cats. Though she never felt the burning desire she had once felt for Peter, she figured having a partnership that was trustworthy, pleasant, and stable was preferable to one of passion, which she associated with drama and selfishness because of her mother. And when Ed confessed to Grace on their second date that he was a divorcee, that his first wife had left him when she found out he was unable to produce offspring, she couldn't help but feel sorry for him. She assured him that she wasn't interested in being a mother. Her PhD was *her* baby.

"Lois and Robert are here for dinner, too," Ed said, interrupting Grace's trip down memory lane. "I saw them on the way back from the bathroom. They're over there by the fireplace."

"Did you say 'hello'?"

"Yes, of course."

"I'll have to go over later. But first, let's order."

"Good idea." Ed flagged down the waitress. "Hi, yes, we'd like to order. I'll have the steak, medium, and a baked potato with sour cream and chives." Grace tried to keep her smile to herself. "And Grace here will have the—"

"I'll have the soft-shell crabs, please." Grace smiled, folded her menu shut, and handed it to the waitress.

Ed did his best to make conversation. He asked Grace if she thought they should refinance their mortgage. And whether she wanted to vacation by the shore that summer. Grace, who was normally quite chatty and asked a lot of questions, simply sat there and listened, chiming in only when necessary. She felt out of sorts and distracted, as if half of her was there and the other half was still lying in Peter's arms. After dessert, a piece of carrot cake that they shared, Ed reached for Grace's hand.

"Honey, is something wrong?" The glare from the

candlelight bounced off the thick lenses of his glasses.

"I'm fine. Just tired I suppose."

"I'm so proud of you. What would I do without you? Just think, you'll have tenure soon, and we'll be completely settled in this beautiful town. I feel like such a lucky guy." His hands felt soft, white collar. He kept his nails trimmed without fail, and was always clean-shaven.

"Thank you, Ed. Fingers crossed. It's not a done deal yet, but at least it's within reach." She pulled her hand away gently. "Should we ask for the check?"

"Okay, sure." Ed flagged down the waitress and reached for his billfold. "May we have the check, please?"

The waitress dropped it off and Ed studied it, carefully calculating the correct tip—not a penny more. Ed helped Grace with her coat and they walked toward Lois and Robert's table. They were still on their main course.

Lois looked up from her plate. "Well, hello there, lovebirds. What's the occasion? I rarely see the two of you out for dinner." She took a sip of her wine.

"Grace is up for tenure," Ed said as he placed an arm around his wife.

"Grace! That's fabulous news! Congratulations." Lois beamed.

"Thank you. It hasn't quite hit me yet."

"Ach, Grace! You're always so humble. You deserve it! Cheers, to Professor Gilmartin!" Lois raised her glass to Robert's and they clinked.

"Here, here!" Robert said. "That'll be front page news tomorrow in the *Gettysburg Times*. Just kidding. Did you see the picture of all of us at the White House dinner in last Saturday's paper?"

"Yes! Front page. Couldn't miss it! People keep stopping me to ask how it was." Grace smiled.

"What a dream, huh? And they had the Everly Brothers play for us live! I even framed our dinner menu and it's hanging in our dining room. Memories to last a lifetime." Lois folded her arms and leaned back slightly in her chair, contented.

"Great idea to frame the menu. Well, we should let you get back to your dinner. Nice to see you both!" Grace turned toward the door. "Goodnight Lois. Bye Robert." Grace and Ed walked out into the starry night.

That night Grace couldn't sleep. She could hear Ed snoring loudly in the next room. She lay there replaying every single move, from the moment her doorbell rang that afternoon. Her heart longed to see Peter again. She felt a connection to him, one she didn't have, and would probably never have, with Ed. She looked over at the clock beside her bed: 2:07 a.m. Crickets chirped outside her bedroom window and the moonlight cast a white light into the room. *Breathe in through the nose three counts, breathe out through the mouth*, she told herself. Just like she used to tell her brother when he couldn't sleep. That didn't work. She tossed and turned, then finally decided to get up. She walked over to her desk, laid out a blank piece of stationery, grabbed a pen and started writing a letter to St. Mary's Maternity Home.

To whom it may concern,
My name is Grace Gilmartin. I resided in St. Mary's
Maternity Home in the spring of
1943 and gave birth to a daughter on June 7 of that year. I realize that it was a closed adoption, but if there is any way I could contact the baby I gave up, or even receive information about her whereabouts or the couple who adopted her, I would be eternally grateful.
Thank you for your consideration.
Cordially,
Prof. Grace Gilmartin

Grace sealed the envelope. She wrote her office address in the top left corner, so there'd be no chance Ed would see the letter should it be returned—or if they sent her a reply. She placed the envelope in her bag so she wouldn't forget it, then settled back down and fell fast asleep.

♠♠♠

Grace and Peter managed to meet up a couple more times. She surprised herself with her ability to be so sneaky, and she was swimming in guilt. First, Peter had left a note in her college mailbox asking her to meet him at the battlefield observation tower closest to her house. Ed was off playing tennis. Peter brought a picnic, complete with champagne and strawberries. As they watched the sun set over the Blue Ridge Mountains, Grace worked up the courage to tell him about the daughter she'd given up years before.

Peter put out his cigarette with his shoe and turned to face her. "What did you mean last time, when you said you didn't go to Quebec?"

"I went to a maternity home."

"A maternity home?" He took her hands in his and thought for a long while. "Was it..."

"It was yours, yes. From that night in the boat-house," Grace said, relieved to hear the words come out of her mouth. "It was my first time. Ever. My only time before Ed. I can't believe I'm telling you this now. No one, I mean *no one*, except for the nurse and my college friend Nancy know about this."

"Grace! Why didn't you tell me?"

"Why didn't I tell you?" The volume of Grace's voice increased, hurt by the memory. "Because of that time on the phone when you were going on and on about how your roommate at Amherst was *trapped* because he'd got a girl pregnant. You said that that was your worst nightmare. You said that you were never getting married. That marriage and kids crushed dreams." Peter put his hands to his head.

"Oh, my God, Grace. I'm so sorry! I was young and so arrogant. Downright stupid."

"It's okay. I mean, it's over. I had the baby and gave it up for adoption. Plus, you're not the only one who had dreams. If I'd kept the baby, I doubt I would have gone on to graduate school and become a professor. I couldn't give up on my own dream, and I wouldn't have wanted you to give up on yours." Grace's eyes filled with tears. Peter pulled her to him and held her tight.

"I'm so sorry you had to go through that alone, Grace! I'm sorry I wasn't there for you."

"Maybe if there hadn't been a war, and you and I weren't so damn ambitious, we'd be living together with our daughter now, somewhere in New England." Grace laughed and wiped her tears away with the back of her hand.

"A daughter?"

"Yes, she was a girl. I held her for all of two minutes before they took her away. She was beautiful. She had your dark hair."

"Oh, Grace. I can't believe it. This is so much to take in."

"I know. That's why I tried to forget it all these years. Otherwise it's just too much."

Peter wrapped a blanket around Grace. Fireflies flickered in the fields below. Grace took a deep breath. The smell of freshly cut grass filled her lungs. "I wish I could hold on to this moment forever."

"Me too, Grace. Me too."

6
The Bridgettes

Tuesday, June 28, 1960

When Grace took the lid off the Tupperware containing the deviled eggs she'd made for bridge club, the sulfur smell made her turn her head in disgust. The mayonnaise mixture must have gotten warm in the car on the way over. Grace thought they would probably still be okay to eat, so she asked Ethel for a platter to lay them out on. Ethel lived on Sunset Avenue in Colt Park, a burgeoning neighborhood at the south end of town. Her home was modest, which was to be expected on her teacher's salary. Wood paneling lined the walls, and she had the latest avocado-colored refrigerator.

The original group of Gettysburg women who had formed the bridge club five years prior called themselves "The Bridgettes." Since then they had grown in

size—they were now up to twelve regular players and
two alternates—but they kept the basic structure the
same. They met religiously at 3:00 p.m. on the first
Tuesday of every month, with the appointed hostess—
they rotated duties—to provide light refreshments,
dessert, and, of course, cocktails. The rest of the girls
pitched in with nibbles and desserts of their own. Jane
was part of the core group and had recruited Lois,
Grace, and, most recently, Olga. Today, it was Ethel's
turn to host. So, like most women in the group, she
went above and beyond to impress their newest member, Barbara Eisenhower, with her desserts—bananas
Foster and pineapple upside-down cake. Three square
tables for four had been set up in the den and covered
with freshly pressed linen tablecloths. A rolling trol-
ley bar waited in the corner, carrying scotch, brandy,
club soda, and ice in a bucket. Percy Faith's 'Theme
From a Summer Place' wafted from the radio.

Grace poured herself a glass of club soda while she
and Ethel waited for the others to arrive. She couldn't
help but think how much had happened since the
White House dinner. She felt like she was on a train
ride with no stops. The initial encounter with Peter
at her home had happened just over seven weeks ago.
Trying to keep it all under wraps the other day at the

country club had been challenging, to say the least.
Here at bridge club it would be even more so. She had
an appointment at Doctor Weikert's office tomorrow,
where she would get the results of her pregnancy test,
but after weeks of sore breasts, queasiness, no period,
and an expanding waistline, she already knew what
the doctor would say.

What the hell was she going to do?! Pregnant,
again, with the same man's child! It was incredible.
She tried to pinpoint which of their secret trysts might
have been the source. Had it been that sunset picnic
on the battlefield observation tower? Or the brief
meeting in his car at the Hotel Gettysburg, while Ike
had been delivering a speech to the local Rotary Club?

Grace had settled into such a comfortable lifestyle
over the years she had spent in Gettysburg: fun girl-
friends, steady and exciting work, a dull-but-happy
marriage. Or had she been denying herself a more pas-
sionate and fulfilling life this whole time? Was this
pregnancy a sign that her life was destined to take a
different course? After all, it wouldn't be the first time
she had gone against the grain. Was she supposed to
choose love and motherhood over her career and her
chosen obligations? Or was it the other way around?
Grace thought back to her favorite book as a child,

one she would often turn to when her parents argued downstairs: *Alice's Adventures in Wonderland*. Alice had had to choose between a small bottle marked "drink me" and a cake iced with the words "eat me". Like Alice, she found herself at a crossroads, unsure of what the outcome of her actions would be. But Alice was a child; Grace was a grown woman.

The sound of ice cubes tinkling in Jane's glass as she mixed herself a drink pulled Grace out of her thoughts.

"Well, hello there, darling! I see you brought your famous deviled eggs. You must share that secret family recipe with me sometime. Ethel told me to bring a pie, so I just grabbed the leftover cherry from Faber's. Nice and easy. Thank God! I just got off work and didn't have time to make anything anyway. Is that club soda? Don't you want me to fix you a proper drink?"

"Yes, please. Pour me some of that scotch. I'll just have one more sip of this." Jane poured her a fresh drink. She looked down at her abdomen and although she could see a slight bulge, she doubted anyone else would notice. Plus, her pleated skirt helped hide it.

Once all the women had arrived and had their drinks in hand, Ethel turned down the radio and faced the group. "Good afternoon, Bridgettes! And a special welcometo our newest member, Mrs.

John *Eis*enhower." Ethel's smile was so big, Grace thought her cheeks mightexplode. Lois looked over at Jane and rolled her eyes. They had joked together the other day about Ethel's strange emphasis on the first syllable every time she said "Eisenhower." "Help yourself to snacks. Now, let's play bridge, ladies! Remember, the winners get $10 cash each, and the losers take home the booby prize—a fruitcake from last Christmas that has been clogging up my freezer."

Everyone had been hovering around Barbara, jockeying for position. Ethel quickly pulled out a chair at her table and invited Barbara to sit down across from her. After all, Ethel was hosting and should have the honor of sitting with their special guest. Grace, annoyed by Ethel's behavior and her nauseating quantity of perfume, looked for a spot at another table, but they'd already been filled. So she seated herself next to Ethel. Olga had already taken the fourth chair.

Ethel cleared her throat. "Barbara and I will be a team, North and South against Grace and Olga, West and East. How does that sound?"

"Fine by me," Olga said, all ready to play as usual, her black ponytail pulled back tightly.

"Sounds good to me, too," Grace said, smiling at Olga.

Grace was an average player. Everything she knew about bridge she'd learned from Lois and Jane.

"Barbara, do you want to be North?"

"Sure, Ethel." Barbara dealt the cards, then opened the bidding for their first game. "One heart." Barbara called out, then took a sip of her drink.

Passing and bidding began. Once the game was underway, the women started chatting between moves.

"So, Olga, remind me again where you're from," Barbara asked, in an attempt to start an easy conversation.

"Richmond, Virginia."

"Oh, I love Richmond!" gushed Ethel, as she held her hand to her heart. "My husband and I stayed at the Jefferson Hotel on our honeymoon. You must have gone there all the time. I just love their bar."

"No, actually, I've never been." Olga said with a straight face.

"What? How could you live in Richmond and never go to the Jefferson Hotel? That's madness." Ethel cackled.

Grace rolled her eyes. She felt bad for Olga, who was still fairly new to town and was being put on the spot by Ethel. She remembered how that had felt when she'd moved to town and stepped in to save her.

"And where do you live now Olga—which part of town?"

Olga kept her gaze on her cards. "We're in Colt Park. A couple of blocks down, on Highland Avenue." She was petite, her skin almost translucent. She wore a rather large amethyst ring, which didn't seem to fit her long slender fingers.

"You know, Colt Park is located on the site of Camp Colt, where my father-in-law was stationed to command the Tank Corps training camp," Barbara said. "That was back when Mamie and Ike still had their first child, 'Icky'. It was a happy time for the three of them, until they lost Ikky to meningitis when he was just three years old. It was devastating. Absolutely devastating." Barbara shook her head and tears welled in her eyes. There was a moment of silence. No one knew what to say. Dabbing her eyes with her hanky, Barbara rebounded. "Oh, my...Let's talk about something pleasant, shall we? I didn't mean to put a damper on the conversation. I'd love to have all you ladies out to the farm for a July Fourth barbecue. How's that for fun?" Barbara smiled brightly at her tablemates.

"Oh, how lovely!" Ethel almost fell off her chair.

"I'll have to give the Secret Service agent your

contact details though, to clear everyone beforehand. It's annoying. But don't worry, it's standard protocol. I think I have everyone in my address book now. Except for you two, Grace and Olga. Why don't you jot down your addresses and phone numbers here for me?" Barbara pulled out a pen and small notepad from her purse.

Grace's ears pricked up at the words "Secret Service agent." *Peter*! By Independence Day, she'd have confirmation that she was pregnant. What would she tell him if she saw him there? Her heart pounded and her palms began to sweat.

"Sure!" Grace took a sip of her scotch, and carefully wrote down her information for Barbara. The stack of tuna salad sandwiches on the table beside her made her stomach churn. She passed the notebook to Olga, and made a bid to keep the game going.

At the table to her right, Grace heard Lois ask, "Is it just me, or is this summer break way too long? I mean, I have the kids signed up for a bunch of camps, but we still have weeks to go until school starts. It's not like the newspaper stops publishing in the summer."

"Oh, I actually love summer with the kids at home." Jane chimed in. "I just give them a bunch of comic books and they hang out at the counter while I'm working."

"Did you sign your kids up for that tennis camp, Barbara?" Lois asked. "Maybe we can carpool!"

Once again, Grace found herself in the position she always seemed to land in, right in the crossfire of mothers talking about their children. Just because she could empathize with what her friends were going through didn't mean she enjoyed hearing about it all of the time! It was a thorny, and mostly boring, subject for her. She wished the conversation could just stick to recent developments in town, like the beautiful new geraniums on the square, or the divine new dress shop that had recently opened on Chambersburg Street. She'd never had anything to contribute when the subject turned to kids. At least so far...

She imagined what it would be like to tell them all, right then and there, that she was expecting. That's right, Grace Gilmartin, thirty-eight years old and pregnant! Take that!

They would, of course, assume the baby was Ed's, and they'd be overjoyed. Hell, they might even pick up her chair like a throne and parade her down the street! But, if they knew it was Peter's, that she had slept with the Eisenhower's Secret Service agent, she would be shunned, never spoken to again. Or was she wrong? Were Jane and Lois loyal enough to stick by her, and keep her secret, as Nancy had?

There was a reason she'd never told her friends in Gettysburg about the baby she gave up years ago at Smith. After her mother left, Grace had had trouble trusting people, women especially—letting them into her life, sharing confidences. Nancy had been the only one she'd trusted with her secret besides Nurse Ruth, and she didn't have any plans to change that.

Grace felt herself becoming increasingly agitated by the conversation around her. "Can we *please* stop talking about kids?!" Grace blurted out.

"Goodness gracious, someone's touchy!" Ethel lowered her chin, pursed her lips together, and looked around to gauge the atmosphere in her living room.

"Excuse me, ladies, I need to use the bathroom." Feeling a rush of nausea, Grace jumped up and went quickly to Ethel's powder room just off the kitchen.

"Now's a good moment for a refill." Jane got up to fix herself another drink. Lois, sensing something was amiss with her friend, made a beeline for the bathroom.

In the powder room, Grace turned on the faucet and left it running, then heaved violently into the toilet. She wiped her mouth with a tissue, leaned on the sink, and stared into the mirror. Tears filled her eyes. What was she going to do? This was the second time a child might enter her life and again the circumstances didn't allow a simple or joyous path ahead for her. Both times, she had been left with a heavy decision to make, all alone.

"Grace? Are you okay in there?" Lois held her ear to the door.

"Yes, yes, I'm fine. Just a little stomach issue. That's all." Grace sniffed and washed her hands. "I'll be out in a second, then it's all yours."

"No rush. Are you sure you're okay? Want me to take you home?"

"No, really, I'm fine."

Grace came out of the bathroom and came face to face with Lois.

"You don't look so hot, Grace. Your face is almost white. Are you sure you're okay?" Grace nodded and went back to her table. Ten minutes later, she felt another wave of nausea come over her.

"Grace, you look like hell. Are you...?" Before Ethel could say another word, Grace leaned over and threw up into her own purse. "Oh, my God! Grace!" Everyone stopped playing and turned toward their table. Jane and Lois got up and hovered around their friend. Lois rubbed her back.

"Sweetie, let's get you outside." Grace nodded, grabbed a napkin, and wiped her mouth as she followed Lois to the screen door.

Ethel leaned toward Barbara. "If I didn't know any better, I'd say she was pregnant." Ethel shrugged her shoulders and waved her hand in front of her face to dispel the lingering smell of vomit. "Please stick around ladies. Let's finish our game."

"Just leave your car here, Grace. I'll take you home." Lois offered. Jane had joined them outside.

"Ethel makes me want to throw up, too, with her brown nosing."

"No, no, I'm fine. Really. Don't worry about me. You just go back in there. I'll take myself home. It's just a five-minute drive. Ed's home. It'll be okay. Promise." Grace slid behind the wheel of her car.

"Grace?" Lois leaned down beside her open car window.

Grace turned on the ignition. "Yes, Lois."

"You know you can tell me anything, right? I feel like you're keeping something from me."

"Yes, of course! It's nothing. Truly. Maybe it was the deviled eggs; you might want to toss them just in case. I'll call you tomorrow." Grace put the car into reverse and backed out of the driveway.

Lois straightened up and placed her hands on her hips. Grace looked at Lois and Jane in her rearview mirror and waved. They waved back with skeptical looks on their faces, then turned to go back inside.

Grace pulled into her driveway, trying to will away another wave of nausea. Once it subsided she went through the back door into the house. She found Ed watching television.

"Grace! You're home early. Everything okay?"

"I'm not feeling so well. I think it was something I ate at bridge. I'm going to go lie down for a while."

"Oh, honey. I'm sorry you're feeling out of sorts. Let me know if I can get you anything."

By 9:00 p.m. that night Grace was in her pajamas and ready for bed. This was her usual routine. It gave her time to catch up on her reading and escape into another world. The stress of her day-to-day life had been manageable until now, because she could always rely on having her own time at the close of each day. Having an infant would disrupt everything—let alone dealing with the social fallout of a broken marriage and an illicit affair. She took pleasure in orderly things—the perfectly stacked piles of clothes in her closet, the tidy row of books on her bookshelf, alphabetized for easy reference. And she loved her solitude in the evenings.

Ever since Peter had come back into the picture, her life had become increasingly chaotic, and she felt herself spinning out of control. In exactly twelve hours, she would receive the test results from her doctor. In bed, she stared at the ceiling, terrified at the prospect of all the decisions she would need to make if the results were positive. There was a soft knock at the door and Grace sat up in bed. Her bedside lamp was still on. "Yes? Come in."

"Are you feeling any better, Grace? I just wanted to check on you before I head off to bed." Ed stood at the door.

"Yes. I'm fine…I just…" Grace couldn't help herself. Tears welled in her eyes. She blinked, causing them to stream down her cheeks.

Ed walked to the foot of her bed and sat down, putting his hand gently on her leg. "Honey, whatever is the matter?"

As much as it killed her to keep the truth from him, she knew she had to. "It's nothing. I'm just tired, that's all. It's been a long day."

Ed moved closer to her on the bed. He held the back of his hand to her forehead, then tucked her hair behind her ear. "You do feel a bit warm. Can I get you anything?"

"That's sweet of you to offer, but no, I'm fine." Ed grabbed a tissue from the box next to her bed and wiped away her tears.

"I'll let you get some rest." Ed leaned in and kissed her on the lips. "Tell me if you need anything, okay?"

"I will. Of course. Thank you, Ed." Grace settled back down and switched off her light.

Ed walked to the door, paused, turned around and said, "I love you, Grace. Goodnight."

"I love you too, Ed," she replied. The door closed softly behind him, and a welcome darkness cocooned her. She felt like the biggest fraud.

When she finally fell asleep, Grace had a haunting dream. She was back at St. Mary's Maternity Home, only this time Ed was beside her in the birthing room, holding her hand and telling her to breathe. Her legs were spread open, her feet bearing down onto cold metal stirrups. A nurse held up a razor and told her it was time to shave "down there." Before she knew it, there was blood spattered everywhere—on her hospital gown, on the thick lenses of Ed's glasses, on the floor. She heard a baby crying, but it was nowhere in sight. A panicked Grace asked

Ed where her baby was, and he answered, "It's okay, Grace. The baby left."

7
The Results

Wednesday, June 29, 1960

Grace awoke to the sound of robins chirping outside her bedroom window. She was unsettled. She slid her feet into her slippers and pulled her robe over her shoulders. She tiptoed past Ed's room, where he was snoring loudly, and made her way downstairs to the kitchen. Sunshine streamed through the bay window, scattering light across their eating nook. Grace glanced at the clock: 7:43 a.m. Ed would be down by 8:15, as he always was, dressed and ready for work, expecting his two eggs, over easy, with rye toast and a cup of coffee, before heading out the door. Grace grabbed the eggs out of the refrigerator as Shakespeare rubbed against her shins, purring.

"Everybody wants breakfast from me, don't they?"

Grace set the eggs down on the counter and filled his bowl with cat food.

Grace would have breakfast on the table for her husband, along with today's *Gettysburg Times*, by the time he came downstairs. Her doctor's appointment wasn't until 9:30 a.m. After that, if she could muster enough concentration, she planned on spending the rest of the day grading her students' final papers.

She went out front to get the newspaper. She held it up to her nose, inhaling deeply; she loved the smell of the fresh ink. She also loved having the first half hour of her day to herself, perusing the paper before Ed tore into it. Today's headlines: "Eisenhower's Planned Trip to Moscow Scrapped" and "Local Man Caught Shoplifting at G.C. Murphy." If you ever did anything illegal in Adams County, the entire town would know about it the next day, if not sooner.

"Good morning, dear. Looks like you're feeling better. Could you straighten my tie for me?"

Grace dropped the paper, as if she had been caught stealing herself.

"Oh, shoot! I haven't started your eggs yet. Sure, come here. You're up early. Did I forget about a morning meeting?" Grace adjusted Ed's tie with a simple tug, then turned her back to him and switched on the stove-top burner. "Go ahead and sit down. I'll get you a cup of coffee."

"Anything worth reading in the paper today?" Ed leafed through the first few pages, skimming the headlines.

"No, nothing in particular." Grace's voice cracked. She found it increasingly difficult to pretend it was a normal day. She felt guilty leaving Ed completely in the dark about what was going on, but she couldn't risk him finding out, not now. If he knew, she was sure he would assume the baby was his. Though he would be ecstatic, albeit incredulous, at the news considering his infertility diagnosis, she predicted he would also assume that she would want to quit her job to stay home with the baby. *Goodbye tenure, goodbye career.* What would she do with a baby anyway? All her friends' children were close to finishing elementary school, if not already in junior high. She would be left to tote her infant around town, excusing herself from conversations to change diapers. Is that what she'd gone to graduate school for? To sit in her backyard, watching a baby crawl around on a blanket? On the other hand, the prospect of motherhood felt like it could satisfy a deep yearning she'd carried with her ever since she had given up her firstborn. Wildly conflicting thoughts like these had been ricocheting around her head for weeks.

"Grace! My toast! It's burning!"

Grace snapped back to reality and removed the blackened toast from the toaster.

"Oh, no! I'm sorry! My head was somewhere else."

"It sure was, but I only have five minutes. Throw in another slice, would ya?" Ed took a loud sip of his coffee and continued to read the paper. Grace rolled her eyes, put another slice of rye in the toaster, and slid Ed's eggs onto a plate. The smell made her stomach turn. Ed wolfed down the food. As he gave her a kiss goodbye, Grace saw a bit of egg yolk on his shirt and told him to hold on. She ran to the sink, wetted a tea towel, then dabbed his shirt gently.

"I'm already running late! Just leave it." Ed swatted her hand away. She took a step back as he grabbed his briefcase. "Where are my car...?" Before he could say another word, Grace handed him his keys. Their marriage worked like clockwork—carefully synchronized, each gear fitting into the next. Sure, it needed some oiling from time to time, but in general it worked.

"Thank you. Where would I be without you, Grace? Are you sure you're okay? You seem a bit off again today. I'm worried about you." Ed started out the back door.

"I'm fine. Just tired, I suppose. Still waking up."

"Well, take it easy and I'll see you when I get home. We don't have any plans tonight, do we?"

"No, I really need to grade those papers. See you later, hon." She waved, then closed the door and let out a long sigh.

Grace didn't want to be too early for her appointment; she couldn't risk anyone she knew seeing her there. If they did, what kind of ailment would she concoct? A sore throat? A rash?

An hour later, Grace arrived at the doctor's office, reported to the receptionist, took a seat in the farthest corner from the entrance, and hid behind an oversized copy of *Good Housekeeping*. There was one other woman in the waiting room, with, presumably, her son. Grace stole glances at them. The boy reminded her of Andrew when he was that age, somewhere around eight. After their mother left, Grace had been the one to take her little brother to the doctor whenever he had the flu or needed a shot.

She really missed Andrew. They had been closer back then than they were now. She was relieved that everything had worked out for him, despite the concerns she had had when they were younger. Kids could be so cruel—she'd seen that firsthand with Andrew. It was torture to watch him endure such teasing. She could only imagine how much more painful it would have been to watch a child go through that as their mother.

But Andrew had gotten lucky and found a loving wife, Anne, straight out of high school, as well as a job managing a grocery store in Lowell. Anne was a teacher, and with their combined income they were able to buy a modest house just blocks away from where he had grown up. Anne and Andrew had two small children, girls. Grace was glad Andrew had chosen to stay in their hometown, and so close to their father. His grandchildren kept him on his toes and brought him joy. Grace would send birthday cards and keep up with their lives during monthly phone calls and they would all get together once a year, at Christmas. Grace and Ed drove eight hours up to Lowell and usually spent two nights with her father, since Andrew and Anne didn't have a spare room. Ed would help George with his finances. Grace would cook a nice Christmas dinner with Anne, using groceries from Andrew's store. The morning after Christmas Grace would do a deep clean of her father's house, then off she and Ed would drive, back to Gettysburg. Andrew had called her a few weeks ago to tell her about an article he'd read about the Jodrell Bank telescope in England. She listened as intently as possible, but had trouble following the technical details that Andrew always seemed to be obsessed by.

"Mrs. Gilmartin?" The nurse called out abruptly, causing Grace to startle. She had made the decision to keep her name back in graduate school because she had already published articles and had wanted to make a name for herself in academic circles. It always irked her when people assumed she went by Mrs. Gilmartin, even though it was a safe assumption and something few ever even thought to question. She could hear her heart pounding in her ears as she followed the nurse to the examining room. Dr. Weikert was at his desk and motioned for her to sit down. He smiled and said, "Good news, Grace! Your blood work came back and it shows a positive pregnancy result."

Grace stared back at him, expressionless. "Grace, are you okay? You don't seem too happy about the news." Dr. Weikert bunched his eyebrows, looking confused. "I mean, it's a miracle in a way—a woman your age getting pregnant."

"No. I mean, yes. It's wonderful news." Grace sat up straight in her chair, and her throat tightened. "Truly."

"Now, although you probably know better than me when this baby was conceived, I would estimate that you're about six to seven weeks along. So I'd say we can expect a bundle of joy to arrive sometime around Valentine's Day. Isn't that a nice thought?" Dr. Weikert's eyes twinkled. Grace vacillated between wanting to strangle him and wanting to hug him.

"Yes, that is a nice thought." Grace bit her lip. Images of her with a protruding stomach in front of a class full of students flashed through her mind. "When do you think I might start showing?"

"Well, seeing as this is your first, probably not until the end of summer or the beginning of fall." Dr. Weikert wrapped a blood pressure cuff around her upper arm, and started pumping. Grace winced as the cuff tightened.

Grace knew it wasn't her first and wondered if she would start to show sooner than that. She thought about her tenure letter. The board was scheduled to meet the week before students arrived on campus, in mid-August.

Dr. Weikert removed the cuff from Grace's arm, and asked her to step onto the scale. He jotted a few notes in his book. "Now, I want to see you back here in about four weeks for a check-up. Be sure to schedule something with my receptionist before you leave. You have the summer off, right? From teaching?"

"Yes. Well, I'm preparing for next semester, but yes, I'm off this summer."

"Well, that's wonderful! You rest up and drink plenty of water, especially during the first few months. It's important, especially at your age."

Grace had never thought, or felt, that thirty-eight was old before, but by the way Dr. Weikert was talking, it seemed she was already a grandmother. "I will. Thank you, Dr. Weikert." Grace left. The mother with the little boy smiled at her in the waiting room. Once the receptionist had hung up the phone, Grace leaned in closer, trying to prevent the other woman from hearing her speak.

"Hello! Yes. Dr. Weikert wants to see me in four weeks."

"Let me see here." The receptionist pulled out a large calendar and flipped to the end of July. "How does July 29 work? That's a Friday."

"Yes, that should be fine. Thank you." Grace glanced out of the corner of her eye at the mother who was watching them.

"And what is it pertaining to?" The receptionist

peered over her glasses, pencil in hand, as the door to the waiting room opened and Ethel walked in.

"Well, my, my, my! What are you doing here, Grace? Is this for your stomach troubles, you poor thing?" Ethel's presence threw the room into a chaotic blur. The stench of her perfume was overwhelming, and Grace sneezed. "Oh, my goodness, you really do have it bad! Bless you, dear."

"Thank you, Ethel. I'm fine," Grace said tightly, then turned back to the receptionist, who was tapping her pencil against her clipboard impatiently. Ethel took a seat across from the woman with the child and picked up a magazine. Grace broke out in a sweat. She tried to think of something quickly, something that wouldn't raise eyebrows. "Just a regular check-up. My iron levels were low. Dr. Weikert did some more blood work, so he wants me to come back for a follow up." No one would question her about low iron levels.

"Alrighty! I have you down at 10:30 on July 29th. See you then, Mrs. Gilmartin."

"It's actually Professor Gilmartin." Grace said.

"Oh. Sorry. Professor Gilmartin."

"See you then. Goodbye. Bye, Ethel."

"Goodbye, Grace. I really do hope you feel better. See you at Barbara's barbecue next week?"

"Yes, I'll be there!"

Grace ran to her car, shut the door, and leaned her forehead against the steering wheel. A vision of the day her mother left came to her—the slamming door, the frosted window, her leather suitcase. She had the instinct to pull out of the doctor's office parking lot and just keep on going, but she headed toward home instead.

Twenty minutes later, when Grace was long gone, Ethel was called back to Dr. Weikert's office. She was having a wart on her foot removed. "I hope there's not a stomach bug going around, or whatever Grace has," Ethel remarked, as she hopped up on the leather examination table and removed her shoes. Before Dr. Weikert had a chance to reply, there was a soft knock at the door. He excused himself and stepped out into the hall to speak with the receptionist, keeping the door slightly ajar.

"I need the blood you drew from Grace to send to the lab," the receptionist said, a little too loudly.

"What? I didn't draw any blood. She's coming back for her next prenatal check-up." Dr. Weikert said quietly.

Not quietly enough. Ethel, ever the snoop, heard every word and her mouth dropped open. She closed

it quickly and regained her composure as Dr. Weikert
stepped back into the room, offering his apologies. He
walked over to the corner of the room to retrieve the No-
vocaine and approached her with a large needle. Normally, Ethel could only focus on the uncomfortable
burning sensation on her foot during these treatments,
but this time she was so taken aback by what she'd just
overheard that she didn't even notice—she was too
busy putting two and two together.

8
Independence Day

July 4, 1960

Grace wasn't the first member of Queens' Row to arrive at the Gettysburg Country Club. She had errands to run and needed time away from her chatty cohorts to just think. She also had a craving for something sweet, so she walked the two blocks from her house to the Lamp Post Tea Room, where they baked fresh glazed donuts each morning. It was an exceptionally muggy Fourth of July—already 88 degrees at 9:00 a.m, with the sun ablaze in the sky. Barbara and John Eisenhower were hosting a barbecue out at the President's farm that afternoon and Grace was a nervous wreck, as Peter was sure to be there. She wanted to tell him about the pregnancy. But at the same time she knew how dedicated he was to his career and to the president. News of a baby could ruin his future, as well as hers. There was so much at stake. Her marriage, Ed's heart—and his pride. He didn't deserve any of this. And there was, of course, her child's destiny to consider. The ball was in Grace's court. She had to get her ducks in a row, but it was all simply too much to bear before noon. She walked down Carlisle Street, licking her fingers while playing out various scenarios in her head. She felt profoundly alone, the same way she'd felt at twenty as she faced her uncertain future in Massachusetts.

When she reached the house, she noticed that the mail had already been delivered. No news from the maternity home yet, but then again she'd only mailed off her letter a couple of days ago. There was, however, a letter from her father. This wasn't unusual. He wrote from time to time, giving Grace little updates: he had painted the fence out back, the price of milk had gone up six cents... A few years back, he'd finally retired and now he spent his days reading the newspaper, playing poker with a couple of his buddies, and visiting with Andrew and his family. Grace felt sorry for him. Everyone felt sorry for him, and he knew it. Thinking about the rejection and hurt he must have experienced when her mother left was horrible.

George never remarried, and he avoided any talk of his former wife like the plague.

Grace thought about what her life would have been like had she stayed in Lowell and never gone off to Smith. She shook her head as she put her father's letter in the drawer of her desk, where she kept all his letters. If she left Ed, would he have the same sorry fate as her father? She couldn't possibly do that to him.

Later that morning, while driving on Lincoln Highway toward the country club, Grace passed a group of Civil War reenactors on Seminary Ridge and thought how horribly hot they must be in their woolen uniforms. She drove past rows of corn, yellow husks popping out of green sheaves, glistening in the sun. She pulled into the GCC parking lot, gathered her things, and headed toward the entrance. She saw mothers with their feet in the baby pool as they watched over their little ones. She saw Mary up in her chair, her sunglasses on. It was crowded at the pool, but that was to be expected on a holiday weekend. Everyone had time off, and it was a scorcher.

Grace wore the baggiest swimsuit she could find, the one with the little hip-length skirt. After signing in, she made her way to Queens' Row, where Jane,

Barbara, and Olga were sunning themselves while they caught up on the latest magazines.

"Hi, Grace! Come, sit here next to me." Barbara patted the lounge chair where Lois normally sat.

"What about Lois?" Grace set her pool bag down at the foot of the lounge chair.

"Oh, she's still down there playing golf." Barbara laughed. "It's not like the seats are assigned."

"I suppose you're right." But she knew Lois better than Barbara did. Lois was very preoccupied with the pecking order and who sat where. Also: Who has lived in Gettysburg the longest? Who has been showing up to events without hostess gifts? Who has been neglecting to mow their lawn? Lois always kept score.

"I'm surprised you're out here, with the big event you're hosting later this afternoon." Grace spread out her towel on Lois' chair so Barbara wouldn't think she was being rude. "I would be an absolute mess!"

"Well, dear, that's the beauty of hosting things at the Eisenhower farm. Everything is taken care of by the staff. There's hardly anything I have to do, except put on lipstick. Plus, I needed to cool off and a pool is the one thing missing at the farm. Speaking of which, does anyone want to go for a dip with me?"

"Yes, I'm melting!" Jane tossed her magazine on the grass beside her chair.

"I'll join you in a sec," Grace said. "I just want to rub some baby oil on my arms first." As Grace applied the oil to her skin, she felt Olga's eyes on her. Grace looked up, but Olga was quick to look away and lift her magazine to cover her face. Grace tried to shake it off, but there was something about Olga that remained a mystery. Maybe it was because she never contributed much to the conversation. Grace had chalked it up to her being the quiet type; no harm in that.

"Wanna join us in the pool?" Grace asked.

Olga kept the magazine in front of her face. "No, that's okay. I'll get in later. You go ahead."

Grace sat on the edge of the pool and let her legs dangle in the water, near where Barbara and Jane were standing. She heard Lois' golf cleats click-clacking toward them and craned her head to look behind her.

"Well, hello ladies! It's a hot one, isn't it?" Lois wiped sweat from her forehead with a hand towel.

"Come join us!" Barbara called out. Lois sat on the chair where Grace had her towel and started taking off her cleats. "Sorry, Lois," Barbara said in a sing-song voice. "Grace is sitting there." Lois looked up, flustered. She was about to say something, but wisely pressed her lips together and moved to the next empty chair. Lois *was* bothered. They didn't know it, but Lois had had a rough week. She was working hard to keep the *Gettysburg Times* afloat. Subscriptions were down, and she was having trouble finding people to buy advertisements. As a result, she had had less time for her social life than usual and it felt like everyone was having fun except her. Lois thought, "Easy for Grace to be everywhere. She has the summers off, lucky son of a gun!"

"Anyone want anything from the snack bar? I'm going to order a big club sandwich after I change." Lois slipped on her sandals.

"Aren't you coming to the barbecue later?" Grace asked, surprised.

"I wish, but I can't. I have too many deadlines at the paper and a lot of our staff are off for the Fourth. That's the downside of being the owner of something. If you want things done right, you have to do it yourself. Right, Olga?"

Olga nodded, but said nothing.

"I'd love a Coke, if it's no trouble." Barbara said.

"Me too, please." Olga looked up at her and tipped her sunglasses so Lois could see her eyes.

"I'm fine," Jane said as she crouched down in the pool so that her shoulders were underwater.

"An ice water would be great, if you can carry all that!" Grace said.

"Yes. No problem." Lois made her way to the snack bar.

Grace slipped into the pool and fully submerged herself. The water felt good against her skin. She thought about the baby growing inside her, how it was swimming in her womb while she swam in the pool. They were like the beginnings of a Russian doll. She'd never imagined motherhood would be in the cards for her, after the adoption, but she was slowly warming to the idea. She had loved her first baby the moment she saw and held her. Her sweet smell. Her tiny fingers. Her soft cheeks. A deep sense of regret washed over her, just thinking about it. She tried to forgive herself, to cut herself some slack and remember why she'd given up the baby to begin with. She had changed so much since then, but the same fears lingered. If she was honest with herself, she was scared of being a mother. Even if the circumstances were ideal, did she have it in her? Her own mother certainly wasn't much of a role model. Grace didn't want to follow in her footsteps, but she had carved out a life for herself on her own terms, just as her mother had done. Grace had thought she was happy, but now she doubted the path that had led her to where she was today. What if the baby growing inside of her was a second chance, a sign, a gift even?

Grace climbed out of the pool, toweled herself dry while trying to hide her changing body, and sat down on her chair. Jane and Barbara joined her and resumed their sunbathing. A few moments later, Grace glanced toward the snack bar window and saw Lois waiting for her order and in deep conversation with Ethel. Ethel looked up toward Queens' Row every few moments, then back at Lois, cupping her hand over her mouth to hide what she was saying. Grace had a sinking feeling.

"What in the world are Ethel and Lois talking about down there?" Grace asked, hoping her friends would put her mind at ease.

"Someone needs to put a muzzle on that woman!" Jane didn't even bother looking up. She was lying comfortably on her stomach, half asleep.

Grace pulled out a book from her bag, to serve as a distraction. Barbara and Jane continued to bake in the sun. Minutes later, Lois arrived with a paper plate groaning under the weight of an enormous club sandwich. Olga had jogged down to help after seeing her struggle to carry all their drinks.

"Oh, thank you so much, Olga! You're a doll for helping me with the drinks." Lois sat down and took a bite of her sandwich.

Barbara watched her kids jump off the high dive, Jane cut out coupons, Lois and Olga buried their noses in their magazines, and Grace lost herself in *The Fountainhead*. When she'd finished the chapter, she looked up and was surprised to see that it was already 2:00 p.m.

"You're not very talkative today, Lois," Grace said, as she took a bag of Utz potato chips out of her bag and stuffed a handful unceremoniously into her mouth.

"Ah, sorry. Just a bit stressed. Glad to see that stomach bug has gone away, though," Lois said, raising her eyebrows.

"Yeah, it must have been a 24-hour thing," Grace replied, as she reached into the bag for more chips.

"Hate to say it, but I gotta go, ladies," Lois said as she began packing up her bag. "Have fun later at the farm."

"We'll miss you, Lois. Good luck with your deadlines. Maybe the barbecue will make headlines," Barbara said.

"You never know," Lois said with a wink, then she walked toward the parking lot without looking back.

◆◆◆

Ed was behind the wheel and Grace sat beside him with her window rolled down all the way, breathing in the fresh-cut-grass smell of summer. Barbara had mentioned there was going to be steamed shrimp and coleslaw at the barbecue, and Grace was starting to get her appetite back. Between her nerves and the morning sickness, she hadn't been able to eat a thing all day. It was a long drive up the tree-lined lane to the Eisenhower farm. But, to get to that point, guests first had to stop at a small, white, wooden outbuilding that served as a security station. And of course, there he was, as handsome as ever. Grace pushed her sunglasses further up on her nose and looked down at her lap, trying to appear as casual as possible while avoiding eye contact.

"Good afternoon, sir. Your name, please?" Peter hadn't noticed it was her in the passenger seat yet; her headscarf helped conceal her identity.

"Ed Kingston and Grace Gilmartin." Ed had his left arm propped on the window, a cigarette between his fingers and his right hand draped over the steering wheel. Peter paused and looked up slowly from his clipboard, his eyes aglow. He ducked his head into the car to look past Ed to the passenger seat. Grace tried to keep her gaze trained straight in front of her.

Peter cleared his throat. "Welcome to you both. Once you get to the end of this drive, hang a left and you'll see plenty of places to park." Peter crossed their names off the list and waved them forward.

"Don't you need to see some form of identification?" Ed asked.

"No, sir. You're on the list."

Ed tipped his hat to Peter as he put the car into drive. "Some Secret Service agent he is," he mumbled as he stubbed his cigarette out in the ashtray.

"It's a private party, Ed. Low security threat." Grace said, defending Peter. "Plus, I don't even think Ike is here today."

As they continued up the lane they passed a horse shelter on the left, next to a small orchard of apple trees. Though they had driven by it hundreds of times, this was Grace and Ed's first time as guests at the First Family's compound.

"This place is huge!" Grace said, as she got out of the car and scanned the grounds. She had heard stories about the Eisenhower farm, but seeing it in person was a whole other story. Since Ike loved golf, he had installed a putting green years ago, complete with a sand trap. There was also a helicopter landing pad, a tea house, and a barn where he kept his cars. But it was also a working farm. Eisenhower maintained a successful cattle enterprise, with about sixty Angus cows—the most notable being the 1,800-pound prize bull named "Black Brutus"—that provided a novel, folksy diversion when world leaders came to visit.

From the parking area, Grace and Ed followed another couple who had just arrived, figuring they knew where they were going. Grace hooked her arm into Ed's, so she wouldn't stumble on the gravel.

"Would you look at that view?" Grace said as she pointed west toward South Mountain.

"It really is quite impressive," Ed conceded. "Ike picked a prime spot."

As they approached the main house, voices and laughter drew them to a large patio where they found Barbara, dressed in a beautiful dark-blue gingham frock, greeting guests as they arrived.

"Ah, Grace and Ed! So glad you could join us! Come over here and let's get you a drink." Barbara waved them over to where everyone was standing. Kids were running around the dandelion-strewn yard, playing tag. The smell of burgers sizzling on the grill wafted through the air. Barbara flagged down one of the wait staff who was carrying a tray of empty glasses. "What will it be?"

"A Manhattan for me, please," Ed said.

Grace looked around to see what other people were drinking. "I'll have the same, please."

Barbara motioned to the young man with the tray. "Coming right up," she said with a salute.

"The president isn't here today, is he?" Ed blurted out, in an attempt to make pleasant conversation.

"No, Ike had business to attend to down in Washington. You know, with everything that's going on now with Russia, he's constantly got meetings and the press to deal with."

"Geez, I know! I don't know how he does it," Ed said. "It's got to be the most difficult job in the world, hands down."

Grace looked over to her right and saw Robert, Lois' husband, talking to Jack and Jane in a loose circle of people. Grace smiled, and waved to him. It was strange to see Robert at a social event without his wife. "Such a shame Lois couldn't be here," Grace remarked.

"I know. It sounds like she has a lot on her plate," Barbara said, crossing her arms. "The budget cuts are really catching up to her. I wish there were some way we could help."

The waiter returned with their drinks. Grace noticed that there was no music playing, which was fine, since there was so much crosstalk. But it did create a rather stiff atmosphere. She glanced around to see if she could spot Peter, and felt her disappointment mounting as she scanned the yard. She handed her drink to Ed and excused herself quietly from the patio area to go in search of the bathroom.

As she passed through the glass sliding doors onto Mamie and Ike's sun porch, Grace saw an easel in the corner, a half-finished oil painting of John and Barbara's children leaning against it. A photograph was taped next to it. Grace assumed that Eisenhower himself had been using the photo to paint from. It was common knowledge around town—and throughout the country—that Ike's favorite pastime, besides golf, cattle, and bridge, was painting. Grace walked over to the easel and leaned in to get a better look at the portrait. The president's only surviving son had produced four children! The thought that the baby in her womb might do the same warmed her heart. The life her own baby could have flashed before her eyes—school, sports, falling in love, career, marriage, Christmases around the fire. A true human legacy. Whether it was loneliness, desperation, or a sense of duty to the truth, whatever it was, after seeing the painting she knew she had to tell Peter about her pregnancy. Grace knew she would regret it if she didn't, and history would only repeat itself. The bathroom could wait. She hurried outside toward the parking area, glancing behind her to make sure no one was watching. When she arrived at the Secret Service security office, she found Peter inside, alone. She pushed through the screen door.

"Grace!" Peter stood up from his desk.

"There's something I have to tell you."

Grace was panting, out of breath. He placed his hands on her shoulders to calm her down. "What's the matter?"

A man in dirt-soiled clothing came through the door. Grace jumped back and Peter dropped her hands. She racked her brain for an excuse, in case it was needed.

"Hey, Peter! I thought you would be down in Washington today," the man hardly looked up at Grace as he filled up his mug with coffee.

"Nope. I'm headed down there tonight, though. Tom's on duty now with the president. They wanted me up here to keep an eye out at Barbara's barbecue. Mamie's upstairs." Peter glanced over at Grace with apologetic eyes. "Grace, this is one of the groundskeepers."

The groundskeeper looked up while lighting his cigarette, finally acknowledging her presence. "Well, hello there, ma'am. Mind if I have a smoke? I'm on my break."

"No, not at all. I was just leaving actually. I was walking around the farm and noticed a light on in this curious little building attached to the barn. Thank you, Peter, for the tour. Now, what's the best way to get back to the patio area?"

"I'll come out with you and point you in the right direction." Peter held the screen door open, then walked Grace away from the building, talking just loud enough for the groundskeeper to hear. "Just head down this path, then past the rose garden toward that windmill." Peter then whispered in Grace's ear, "Meet me in the barn before you leave, okay?" Grace nodded.

Peter went back into the office.

"She was a pretty thing." The groundskeeper blew out a cloud of smoke, then took a sip of his coffee.

"One of the guests. People are always getting lost out here. Can't blame them."

After they'd eaten their potato salad and burgers, and watched the kids catch fireflies in jars and draw their names in the air with sparklers, Grace and Ed decided to make an exit. Half the guests had already left. They walked slowly to the parking area, past the main house and toward the barn where President Eisenhower kept his cars.

"Ed, you go ahead to the car. I'm going to use the ladies room one last time."

"Oh, come on, Grace. Can't you hold it? It's only a 10-minute drive home."

"Sorry, Ed. No. You go ahead. I'll be right there!" Grace turned and walked toward the house until she was sure Ed had rounded the corner. She spotted Peter walking alongside and then into the barn. Grace rushed across the lawn to join him. She shut the barn door behind her and dust particles floated through the air in the last gasp of twilight.

Peter took her hands in his and looked at her searchingly. "Grace, what is it you wanted to tell me?"

"Peter, I'm, I'm pregnant." Grace moved her gaze from down at the ground to Peter's eyes. "And it's not Ed's. It's ours."

"Oh, my God, Grace! I don't know what to say…I…"

"Forget it! Forget I even told you." Grace turned to leave. Peter grabbed her hand and pulled her back.

"Grace, no, please! I'm sorry. I didn't mean that in a bad way. I'm just surprised. That's all. We'll figure this out, okay? Together." He pulled her in tightly.

Tears rolled down her cheek onto his uniform. For the first time in a while she felt protected, as if someone was on her side.

"What are we going to do, Peter?" Silence filled the room as Peter held her tight. "Maybe this child is meant to be. I mean, it *is* the second time this has happened. Maybe it's fate."

Peter took a step back and placed his hands on her shoulders. "Maybe." There was a strange mix of joy and sadness in his voice, as if he was still processing the gravity of the situation.

Grace looked up at him. "But what in the world are we going to do? I'm married, for Christ's sake! I'm up for tenure. You're a Secret Service agent. I mean, it doesn't get any more complicated than that!"

Peter took Grace's face in his hands and looked her into the eyes, "We're going to make it work this time, Grace. This time we're in it together. I promise."

"Ed's waiting for me. I better get back, otherwise he'll be suspicious." Grace kissed Peter on the lips and walked to the door. She turned and looked at him and thought he seemed sad. She felt bad for dumping such heavy news on him only to walk away in a rush. But she was also relieved that she had mustered up the courage to tell him.

9
The Member Guest

Saturday, July 9, 1960

"Well, I'll be damned!" said Swifty, a gas station owner in town, as he picked up the *Gettysburg Times* and read the front page headline: "Eisenhower's Secret Service Agent—Gettysburg's Most Eligible Bachelor." Now, if there's one thing Swifty had in common with Pastor Mark at the Presbyterian Church, Harry Carmichael at the pro shop, and Dorothy at the ice cream parlor, it was that he *loved* a juicy story. And on this particular Saturday morning, the same morning as Gettysburg Country Club's Member Guest Event, less than a week after Barbara Eisenhower's July Fourth barbecue, the nosy nellies in town got a whale of a tale. Most folks in Gettysburg had a freshly rolled-up newspaper waiting for them on their doorsteps. And the people who didn't subscribe to the paper would hear the news soon enough from their neighbors.

As Grace bent down to pick up her copy that morning, she waved at Cathy Comstock who was walking by with her poodle. But Cathy did not return her wave, as she usually did. Grace thought this incredibly odd, if not rude. Nevermind.

Grace picked up the paper and started reading on her doorstep. Ed was still upstairs in bed. She spread the paper out in front of her and her jaw dropped as she read the headline and accompanying article:

"On May 13, one of President Eisenhower's Secret Service agents was seen leaving the home of a local female in the middle of the afternoon. Approximately six weeks later, the same woman was spotted at a local doctor's office receiving the results of a pregnancy test. The information, obtained from an anonymous source, is under further investigation."

Grace walked over to the breakfast nook, sat down and read the article three times, trying to convince herself that she wasn't dreaming. How could this be? Then it hit her...of course: Terrible, seething, good-for-nothing

Ethel! Grace thought back to that day at the doctor's office, when Ethel had poked her nose in, and then later, at the club, when Ethel had cupped her hand to Lois's ear. Of course it had been Ethel! Who else? But Lois? Why would Lois, her dear friend for all these years, publish such a salacious story—especially without giving Grace the courtesy of a forewarning? Then Grace remembered Lois driving by the day she scooted Peter out the door. She heard Ed coughing as he came downstairs and quickly folded the paper and placed it under her seat cushion. There was no way she could let him see this.

"Good morning, sunshine." Ed shuffled over to the percolator and filled the mug Grace had placed there for him. "It's a beautiful day for golf, isn't it?" He made his way over to the table where Grace was sitting.

"It sure is." Grace cleared her throat. "Though I heard on the radio yesterday that thunderstorms are expected. Hopefully everyone will be finished with the tournament and in the clubhouse for dinner by the time they roll in."

"No paper yet?" Ed scanned the table and countertops.

"Ah. Nuh-uh. Isn't that strange?" Grace shifted her weight to cover the evidence, while Ed walked to the door to check the front porch.

"No news is good news, that's what they say," Grace called cheerfully, as she pushed the paper toward the back of the bench, so no part of it would stick out. "Want me to make you some eggs?" She got up and grabbed a frying pan.

"I want something to read." Ed grumbled, as he continued pacing around the room.

The phone rang. It was Lois, calling to ask Grace if she'd seen the paper yet. Ed was within earshot, so Grace told him she'd take the call upstairs. She set down the receiver, then ran upstairs to their phone on the landing.

"Okay Ed, you can hang up now. I got it." Grace heard a click as Ed hung up the receiver downstairs.

"Grace! I'm so sorry!" There was an anxiousness in Lois' voice.

"For what? What the hell is going on, Lois?"

"I wanted to tell you sooner, I really did. But there was pressure on me to get a story out and meet our publishing deadline." Lois let out a deep sigh. "The *Washington Post* called me two days ago at the *Gettysburg Times* to confirm details of a story they were hoping to publish concerning one of Ike's Secret Service agents. They'd received an anonymous call from a woman in Gettysburg."

Grace swallowed hard. "Does this have anything to do with Ethel?"

After a moment of silence, Lois blurted, "Yes. She came up to me last week at the snack bar and told me she'd seen you at the doctor's office. I drove by your house one afternoon and thought I saw a man leaving. Look, I don't know what's true. I didn't give the *Washington Post* any information. Robert pressured me to run the headline in order to get our subscriptions back up. Ethel told the *Washington Post* that the woman was a college professor. I left that part out."

"Well, I can assure you that it's not me, Lois!"

"Okay. I believe you, Grace."

"I gotta go. I need to make Ed's breakfast, or he'll be late for the Member Guest."

"Will I see you out there, Grace?" Lois sounded sheepish.

"I'm behind on grading papers, but I'm going to try to make it out there in time for dinner."

"Okay. Hope to see you tonight."

Grace said nothing and hung up the phone, then she went back down to the kitchen.

"Everything all right?" Ed asked. "Who was that calling?"

"Lois. She wanted to know whether I was coming to the Member Guest." Grace put on an apron. "Ed, is Charlie coming here first, or are you meeting him out at the club? Registration starts at 9:30. They want to get everyone out there before it gets too hot." Charlie Lewis had been Ed's roommate in college. He was driving up from Winchester, Virginia, where he lived, to partner with Ed for the Member Guest. This was the biggest day of the year for the men of Gettysburg Country Club. It was a chance to play the game they loved and show out-of-town guests the town they loved, all while enjoying cold beers. This year the event would be elevated, as President Eisenhower himself would be participating. It was Ike's fourth Member Guest tournament in a row.

"He's meeting me out at the club. Is the guest room ready for him for tonight?"

"Yes, the bed is all made up and I opened a window. Now, how about some eggs? Otherwise you'll be late."

Behind her calm façade, Grace was going crazy. What the hell was she going to do? Ethel would be at the tournament and she never wanted to see Ethel's face again! If it was up to her, she would skip the whole thing. Peter would most definitely be there, to protect the president as he made his way around the course. They'd left things so open-ended at the barbecue, and now, with the newspaper article, she had no idea where they stood. What a mess!

Grace cracked an egg and the yolk broke and spilled into the pan. She tossed it into the trash can and cracked open another. God! She wished that newspaper headlines could be removed that easily. Chucked away in the trash, erased.

Ed left the house grumpy, mumbling irritably about not being able to read the paper. After pacing around the house, walking into rooms only to forget why she'd gone in in the first place, Grace eventually gathered the focus to get dressed. Maybe if she held her head high and kept her cool, attending the Member Guest would be the best thing she could do right now. She wasn't going to let Ethel win. Plus, if she didn't show up at all, it would deepen people's suspicions—if they'd had any to begin with. Folks would surely be more interested in the president than in her anyway. She zipped up her off-the-shoulder white eyelet summer dress, which showed the tan lines from her swimsuit but was baggy enough to hide her rounding stomach. Her hands shook as she combed her honey-colored hair and stared into the mirror of her vanity table.

Would she make a good mother? Did she really have what it took? The way she saw it, she had three options. The first, safest, and easiest would be to say the baby was Ed's and tell Peter not to worry, that it couldn't be his—that he should continue with his own life and forget this had ever happened. The second option? She could try and get an abortion. But from what she'd read and heard, that option was full of risk, not to mention expensive, and difficult to arrange. The third option would be to choose the man who felt like her soul mate. She allowed herself a moment to imagine what it would be like to just drop everything—her prospects for tenure, her husband, her home on Broadway, her friends—and run away with Peter. Where would they go? Could they go live in some obscure place in New Mexico and open up a bookstore together? Maybe she could get a teaching job at a high school somewhere and Peter could work as a cop. And what about Ed? If she said the baby was his and he believed her, she would almost surely have to resign herself to becoming a housewife—instead of making breakfast every morning for Ed, she would be making breakfast for Ed and "their" child. Or, she could tell Peter the baby was his, but raise it as Ed's, and arrange regular secret meet ups with the child's real father at the playground, or out by Devil's Den on the battlefield. As the various scenarios played out in her head, the phone rang again. She caught it on the sixth ring.

"Hello?" Grace said, out of breath.

"Hi, Grace! It's Nancy." It felt amazing to hear that warm and familiar voice on the other end of the line—just the surprise Grace needed.

"Nancy? Oh, my goodness, you have no idea how much I've missed you! How are you?!" Grace said, her eyes filling with tears.

"I'm good, thanks. I received a message to call you and couldn't wait to ring you back. How are you doing, my dear?"

"Thank God you called. I'm in such a bind, and this time I honestly don't know how to escape it. You're also the only person who could even possibly understand."

After their days at Smith were over, Nancy and Grace had spoken every couple of months for quite a few years. Then, as life got busier, their communications had reduced to annual Christmas letters and the occasional weekend together. Nancy was a through-line for Grace and the sole person she felt she could truly trust, through thick and thin. Nancy lived in Boston, with her husband and two children. She'd become a nurse.

"Well, why didn't you call me sooner?" Nancy asked sternly.

"I don't know. I should have. I guess I was trying to figure things out on my own. You would think a grown woman could do that, wouldn't you? But Nancy, you'll never believe the situation I'm in now. You remember Peter?"

A pause. "Of course I do."

"I know this sounds crazy, but I ran into him at a White House dinner last spring."

"Wait, back up. You went to dinner at the *White House*? How come I didn't know about any of this? And I thought Peter was dead!"

"I know, I'm sorry. A lot has happened since we last spoke. Just bear with me. I thought I had seen Peter here in town once, before the dinner, but I convinced myself that my eyes must have been playing tricks on me. Then I ran into him at the White House. He's Ike's personal security guard."

"Oh, wow! Really? That's crazy."

"Right. So I ran into him and we talked briefly. He

hasn't changed one bit. Just as handsome as before."

"Mm, hmm."

"Then a week later he shows up on my doorstep! Ed was out, thank God. One thing led to another and..."

"And?...Grace?"

"Let's just say, history repeated itself."

"Oh my God, Grace! And this bind you're in?..."

"I...I'm pregnant—and Peter is the father, again."

"Oh, sweetie! I'm driving down now."

"What? No, Nancy! It's very sweet of you, but I think it might make Ed suspicious. No. I need to sort it all out for myself this time. It feels good to tell someone 'safe' though. You know?"

"Oh, Grace!"

"I know. It's a mess. Sometimes I wish I'd just stayed in Manhattan. It seems no one cares about this kind of stuff in the big city. But in small towns? Everyone knows each other's business. My neighbors have nothing better to do than gossip."

"What are you going to do?"

Grace sighed. "I honestly don't know. Got any advice?"

"Follow your heart? That's always helped me."

"But my head gets in the way," Grace sighed. "And to complicate matters even further, I'm up for tenure."

"Grace, that's amazing news! I mean that you're pregnant is also amazing news, but tenure? You've always dreamed of that! Maybe the best thing to do is just to say the baby Ed's, although that doesn't solve your tenure problem. This is a tough one, honey. I don't envy you."

"I know. Ugh, Nancy, I gotta run. The Member Guest Golf Tournament at GCC is today. Much as I dread going, I have to keep up appearances, for Ed's sake. To make matters worse, Peter will most likely be there. Hopefully most people will be so distracted by Ike and Mamie that they won't even think about this morning's headline."

"Wow, you lead quite the glamorous life for a small town girl, Grace. Promise you'll call me if you need anything? Anything at all. I'm only an eight-hour drive away. Six hours by train."

"Thank you, Nancy. I'll let you know. Bye, Mopsy."

"Bye, Flopsy."

Grace hung up the receiver and looked down at Shakespeare. "Well, puss, I guess it's time to get this show on the road."

♥♥♥

The brass rooster weathervane of the clubhouse pointed southwest, where ominous clouds were gathering against an ink sky. Grace pulled into the CountryClub parking lot and saw golf carts parked haphazardly across the manicured golf course. She also saw Ike's 1955 Chrysler Crown Imperial Derham limousine parked just outside the pro shop, next to the putting green. Grace took a deep breath. She needed to ease into this. Picking up her name tag and signing in at the pro shop seemed a good approach. The men would have been out playing all day, and most of the women would have arrived a while ago for pre-round drinks at the clubhouse. A bell tinkled as she opened the door. No one was there, except for local golf pro Harry Carmichael. She walked over to the cash register, where he was cleaning golf balls.

"Hello there, Grace! I thought you'd be out here earlier to watch Ed teeing off with his guest, what's his name?"—Harry scanned the list of names in front of him—"Charlie."

"Unfortunately I had some errands to do."

"Well, at least you made it in time for the awards ceremony. Ed's doing pretty well out there, from what I hear. They're just one hole ahead of Ike."

"Oh, wow! That's great to hear!" Grace said, even

though she wished it were the other way around. If Peter were accompanying the president *ahead* of Ed, she'd be able to see him come off the course first, and maybe even get a chance to speak with him in private. How much time was there between holes? Five minutes? Ten?

"Hey, Gettysburg's most eligible bachelor is out there with Ike, ya know?" Harry looked up at her and smiled. "That was some headline in the paper today!"

Grace's face flushed red. "Well, I'm already taken. Don't I need to sign in?"

"Yes. I'll cross your name off. Here, write your name on this. I expect everyone in the clubhouse will be making their way down here soon for the awards ceremony before heading up to dinner, if you want to stick around."

Grace's breasts were so tender it hurt when she pressed her name tag to her dress. She normally wrote her title, "Prof.," in front of her name, but tonight she was just "Grace."

"I think I'll go grab a drink and bring it down to the patio for the ceremony." Grace glanced out the window of the pro shop and saw that the clubhouse was abuzz with activity. She heard thunder in the distance.

"You'd better hurry. I can imagine the ceremony will be short, with this storm rolling in," Harry said, placing the polished golf balls into a silver bucket by the cash register.

Grace walked up the path to the clubhouse, where all the women had gathered to wait for their husbands. The air was hot and humid, and the wind was picking up, carrying with it the sweet, pungent aroma that presages a coming storm. The country club staff were getting ready for the buffet dinner. A man in a chef's hat was sharpening his knife at a carving station. The sight of the big slab of beef under the red heat lamp made Grace nauseous. There were pies and cakes, presliced on plates. She walked toward the bar, keeping her gaze straight ahead. It felt like all eyes were on her, but were they? She could hear women whispering to each other, and there was the occasional cackle of laughter, but that wasn't so unusual the more she thought about it. There must have been close to fifty women in the room.

Grace held her head high and walked up to the bar. "I'll have a scotch on the rocks, please," she said.

"Grace! You're late. I was wondering when you'd get here." Grace turned to find Jane and Olga directly behind her. Jane wore a look of concern. "Are you okay? You don't look so hot. Did you read the headline in today's paper? Everyone in town is talking about it.

He's here you know, Gettysburg's most eligible bachelor."

"Not now, Jane," Grace replied, shaking her head. "I'm sorry. I just can't…" She raised her glass to her friends. "Cheers! To the Member Guest Event! And to President Eisenhower!"

"Cheers." They clinked glasses. Grace sipped her drink slowly while glancing around the room, trying to find Lois. She spotted her in a corner, talking to a bunch of women, her back to Grace. "We better get outside," Grace continued. "The award ceremony will be starting any second now."

"What time is it?" Jane asked as she glanced down at her watch. "Oh, my gosh, it's 5:15 already! Yes, let's go, or we'll miss it. I want to see Ike pulling up in his golf cart."

"If you'll excuse me," Olga said, "I need to powder my nose first. I'll meet you down there." She was in such a hurry that she bumped into Grace.

"Geez, Olga! You nearly knocked me over." But Olga just made a beeline for the restroom, clutching her large black bag to her body without so much as an apology.

"What's gotten into her?" Jane asked.

"No idea," Grace replied, still a bit stunned.

Jane and Grace followed the parade of summer dresses down the hill to the patio next to the pro shop. Flagsticks were flapping in the breeze at the last hole, 200 yards away. The men lined up their putts and sank them with various degrees of ease. After a round of shoulder-patting and hand-shaking, the men hopped into their golf carts and drove the last 200 yards to the patio area where the crowd was waiting. Harry went around, collecting score cards. The crowd formed a disorganized U-shape under a large dark-green awning, waiting for the president's cart to come in. Supposedly, Ike had received an urgent phone call that had delayed his start time on the final green. Ed spotted Grace and walked over to her with Charlie; both men had smiles on their faces.

"That T-Line putter was the best investment I've ever made," Ed said good-naturedly. Charlie laughed and slapped him on the shoulder.

Ed leaned in to give Grace a kiss on her cheek. "Hi, honey."

"Hi, Ed. Hello, Charlie. How did you fare out there?" Grace wiped the sweat off her glass with a cocktail napkin. She gazed past them to the last hole, where Ike was walking next to his caddy, with Peter following closely behind.

"Not bad. Charlie and I scored 75. We played 'Better Ball,' so the lowest score between the two of us is what counts. Charlie scored a 5, and I scored 4."

"Not bad. I still don't understand how a score of 4 means 75," said Grace, who knew next to nothing about the sport, despite having been a member of the club for ten years.

Harry carried out three trophies, for first, second, and third place, and set them on a table at the front of the room. Grace saw someone from the *Gettysburg Times* holding a camera; likely covering the event just to snag some photos of Ike. As the president approached the green, women smoothed their hair in a futile attempt to combat the wind and humidity, and men straightened their backs and puffed out their chests. Grace could see that Lois was avoiding eye contact with her, as was Ethel. Then, as she continued to scan the crowd, Grace spotted Peter. Her heart beat faster as he approached, her body belying the poise she was trying to maintain in his presence. When he got closer she was the only one in the crowd whose eyes weren't trained on the president. Their gazes met. Lois witnessed this moment—Peter's dark eyes meeting Grace's and Grace smiling back. For a brief moment, Lois and Grace also met each other's gaze. Lois looked sad, regretful. Peter was a few feet behind Ike as he walked toward the crowd. Cameras flashed, and thunder rumbled in the distance. Harry called everyone's attention by clapping his hands together.

"Okay, folks, let's get started so we can get you all up to the clubhouse before this storm hits. Mr. President, if you wouldn't mind standing just over here while I announce the winners." Ike moved closer to Harry, Peter still two steps behind. He glanced over at Grace every thirty seconds or so, as though he was checking on her, making sure she was okay. She was sure he must have read the headlines. "Third prize, with a score of 75, goes to Ed Kingston and his guest, Charlie Lewis, from Winchester, Virginia!" The crowd erupted into applause as Ed and Charlie collected their trophy. Harry continued, looking down at the scorecard and consulting with his colleague to make sure he had it right. "And second prize goes to..." There was a scream from the crowd, "Oh, my God—She has a gun!" The scene was pure panic, as Grace watched everything play out before her in slow motion. She saw heads turn. Then she saw Olga, who was pointing a gun directly at the president.

10
Crossroads

Friday, July 15, 1960

Grace watched the funeral on her small black-and-white television in the den. Ed was at the office.

An American flag was draped over the mahogany casket. The camera zoomed in on a portrait of Peter in uniform alongside a cascade of white lilies. The nation watched as "The Hero Who Saved the President's Life," as had been declared in *The Washington Post*, was given a proper military burial in Arlington National Cemetery. Supreme Court justices, the director of the CIA, a few foreign dignitaries, and, of course, the president himself were all in attendance. It had been Peter's dream to serve his country, and his service had earned him a place in the most hallowed ground in the U.S. His obituary mentioned two sisters and a mother, but

noted that Peter Bowers left behind no wife or children. *Little did they know*, Grace thought.

Grace was drenched in grief. Gradually, she became unreachable, sullen. There were times when her
heartache seemed so much to bear that she was worried her sadness might cause a miscarriage. Most days,
since Peter had been killed, she couldn't bring herself
to eat or sleep. Visions of the shooting played out over
and over again in her head—the look on Peter's face as
he leapt to cover the president, his body crumpling to
the ground, members of the crowd screaming, pushing, running, ducking. It had all happened so fast, yet
the images were still so vivid in Grace's mind.

Harry had grabbed President Eisenhower by the
arm and rushed him into the pro shop. Charlie Lewis,
Ed's friend, shoved Olga to the ground, while Ed himself managed to wrench her arms behind her back
until the police arrived—a throwback to his wrestling
days. Now the town considered him something of a
hero. Even Lois got in on the action, kicking the gun
out of Olga's hands so she couldn't fire another shot.
A Russian spy, in their midst, all along. "She had no
accent!" Jane said, when she was interviewed for the
paper. "And she was a member of our bridge club—
one of our star players!"

The whispers that had hinted at Grace's romance with Peter were soon forgotten. Like a storm that had passed without causing any obvious damage, it was never mentioned again. The townspeople were more preoccupied with the near-assassination of the president, like the rest of the country. Despite the relief Grace felt at no longer being fodder for the town's gossip mill, the fact was that Peter, the father of her child, was gone and was never coming back.

Having learned this lesson from literature, Grace realized that, because of the illicit nature of her love affair, she had to go on with her life as before. When the funeral was over, she got up from the couch and lumbered upstairs to shower. She let the warm water flow over her face and mingle with her tears as she sobbed.

Afterwards, she was so tired that she felt compelled to nap. Downstairs, the phone kept ringing, keeping Grace from dozing off. She went to the kitchen, knocked the receiver off the hook, and crawled back into bed. A couple of hours later there was a soft knock at her bedroom door. She looked over at the clock next to her bed. It read 5:02 p.m.

"Grace, honey, are you okay? I called and called, but kept getting a busy signal."

"I'm fine, Ed. I just needed to catch up on sleep, so

I took the phone off the hook. It's all been too much since the shooting."

"I know. Terrible. Just terrible. I forgot to tell you that Nancy called yesterday. She asked if you could call her back."

"Okay, thank you. I will." Grace sat up on the edge of her bed and stretched her arms up over her head, yawning.

"I'm headed out to the Rotary Club. They want me to give a talk about how we took Olga down. I'm their guest speaker." Ed adjusted his tie in front of the mirror. "I'll be home around 7:00 for dinner... What are we...?" Ed stopped short, realizing this wasn't the time to ask Grace what was for dinner. "I'll pick up a few of those TV dinners on the way home."

Grace nodded. "Sounds like a good plan. Thanks, hon." Ed closed the door and she listened to his footsteps as he made his way downstairs and out the back door. She didn't move until she heard the car start and back out of the driveway.

She decided that she needed to get out of the house for some fresh air and got dressed; a walk would be good for her. She walked down the alley, past the college tennis courts, and up the hill to the observation tower on Oak Ridge, where she and Peter used to meet. Grace climbed the metal stairs to the top of the tower. From now on, she decided, this would be the place she'd come to remember Peter. It would be a secret that was just theirs. When she reached the top, she inhaled deeply and looked out over the McClean Barn, which had been used as a Civil War hospital. Its deep red color contrasted sharply with the lush green grass surrounding it.

It had been six days since the assassination attempt. Six days since Peter had died. Six days of tears and wondering what to do next. Grace was now in her ninth week. In two weeks she had her next check-up with Dr. Weikert. Ed had been so caught up in the media whirlwind following the assassination attempt that, even if he suspected something, he wasn't letting on. He'd tried to comfort Grace, often mentioning how lucky they were that they hadn't been hurt. They both marveled at how no one had even remotely suspected that Olga had been a snake in the grass all along.

As she continued riding the wave of grief, Grace considered her options. The most reckless scenario that Grace had fantasized about—running away with Peter—was no longer an option, so now it was either seek an abortion or lie to Ed and say the baby was his owing to some medical miracle. When Grace had asked her, Nancy had advised against an abortion; her nursing experience told her it was never a good idea unless it was performed by legitimate doctors in sterile conditions. There was a third option, and one she hadn't yet considered. She could divorce Ed, tell him the baby wasn't his, then raise it on her own.

Grace leaned over the rail of the observation tower as she weighed her future. She looked up at the sky, asking Peter for guidance, then backed away from the rail and spread her hands softly over her growing stomach. "Hey, you in there," she whispered. "I don't know whether you're a boy or a girl, but I want you to know, your father was a hero." She swallowed the lump in her throat and wiped away her tears with the palms of her hands.

It was time to get back. Grace descended the steps and made her way back down the hill. It was scattered with downy white puffballs that had once been bright-yellow dandelions. She remembered plucking these from the fields as a child whenever she faced a tough decision or big opportunity. She would blow as hard as she could, watch the seeds scatter, then throw the stem with all her might into the air, hoping her wish would come true.

Grace selected the tallest and fluffiest one she

could find and held it out in front of her, closing her eyes solemnly. "I wish to God that I make the right decision." She watched the seeds waft away across the field, threw the stem up as far as she could, and turned to go home.

♠♠♠

When Grace arrived at her home, she found a surprise waiting for her on the front porch. "Nancy?! What on earth are you doing here?" Grace walked up and threw her arms around her. The release Grace felt at seeing her old friend brought on another round of tears.

"Didn't Ed tell you that I called?"

"Yes. I was going to call you back..."

"I called yesterday to let you know I was coming. But when I couldn't get a hold of you, I hopped in my car and drove down. I tried calling again from a pay phone, but..."

"I'm sorry. I must have been taking a nap."

Nancy squeezed her friend's hand. "Grace, I'm so sorry about Peter. About everything. You poor thing." Grace started sobbing. "Come," Nancy said, leading her to the door. "Let's go inside."

Grace recounted the entire saga for Nancy as they sat facing each other on the sun porch. They talked for a good hour before Ed came home. When he did, he said a quick "hello" and let the two friends continue catching up. Later, when he realized it was getting dark, he slid a dish from the freezer into the micro-wave without interrupting them. Grace heard the mi-crowave ding and Ed called out, "Dinner's ready!"

Grace was touched. It was a small gesture and a simple meal—it was rare for Ed to take care of domes-tic chores like this—but she felt cared for, loved.

"We can eat in the kitchen," Ed said, as he spooned macaroni and cheese onto three plates.

"Do you mind if we turn off the TV?" Grace asked. "I don't think I can stomach hearing any more news about the assassination attempt." Grace's eyes were still puffy from crying all afternoon.

"Sure thing, hon. Geez, Grace, this whole event has had quite an effect on you! You and Nancy go ahead and sit down; I'll bring the plates over."

"Nice to see you again, Nancy," Ed said, smiling. "If we'd known you were coming we would have made a real dinner."

"No apologies necessary! I did show up unan-nounced. I was just so worried about Grace," Nancy said as she rubbed Grace's back. "I had to drive down and check on her."

"You're a good friend," Ed said. "*Bon appetit.*"

"*Bon appetit.*" Grace took a bite of her macaroni. After eating so little the entire week, she found herself shoveling bigger and bigger bites of the warm cheesy mess into her mouth. Soon, her plate was clean.

"Whoa, Grace. Take it easy!" Ed said, feigning surprise. "Glad you like my cooking," he added with a wink.

"Sorry, I was starving!" Grace wiped her mouth with a napkin and set her fork down.

"Well, you're eating for t..." Nancy almost blew her cover. Grace's eyes grew wide and she kicked her under the table. Nancy coughed nervously and took a sip of her water. Grace was terrified her friend would spill the beans before she had a chance to figure out the best path forward. She was tired of keeping her secret from Ed; It wasn't fair to him. She paused, gathering courage, then sat up straight and looked directly at him. "Ed...there's something I want to tell you." Ed froze, mid-bite.

"What is it, Grace?"

"I need to use the restroom," Nancy said. She was smart enough to know her cue to leave.

Ed looked expectantly at Grace, waiting for her to speak. "Grace? What do you want to tell me?" He looked worried.

This was it. It was now or never. The words seemed to stick in her throat. Once she had uttered them, there would be no turning back. She had lost the love of her life, *twice*. And now, with the possibility of a child in her future, her tenure was at stake. She had already lost so much, would she lose the one thing she had worked so hard for?

"Ed, I'm pregnant."

Ed dropped his fork as well as his jaw.

"You're kidding me! Grace! Is this some kind of joke?" Ed asked, incredulous, as he stood up from his chair. "Grace, seriously, if this is some kind of joke?"

"No, it's not a joke. I really am pregnant."

"Grace….Grace! This is wonderful! This is the best news I've ever heard *in my life*! But I'm…I can't… how is it possible? I can't believe it!" Ed took off his thick-rimmed glasses and wiped his eyes with his napkin. Grace had gone over this scenario hundreds of times in her head. She and Ed didn't have sex very often, maybe once a month. After all, they slept in separate bedrooms. But they had slept together the night before the White House dinner, which made her news plausible, despite Ed's diagnosis all those years ago.

"The doctors were wrong, honey! *We're going to be parents*! Our little miracle baby!" Ed helped Grace out of her chair. She placed her hands in his; they felt warm and soft. He pulled her to him and hugged her tightly. A button on his shirt pressed against her cheek as he stroked her hair. "You've made me the happiest man alive, Grace. I'm going to be a father! You're going to be a mother—a wonderful mother."

"That's right. I'm going to be a mother." When Grace said it out loud, it felt strangely comfortable, like a pair of worn slippers. She said it again: "I'm going to be a *mother*. We're going to be parents."

Nancy rapped softly on the kitchen door and stuck her head into the room.

"You knew, didn't you, Nancy?" Ed looked up and smiled. "That's why you're here, isn't it?"

Nancy raised an eyebrow at her friend as she walked toward the table. Grace nodded. "That's right. As soon as I heard the news, I drove down. Her secret is out!" Nancy gave Ed a hug. "Congratulations, Ed!"

Ed spent the rest of the evening close to Grace, making sure she was comfortable, asking if she wanted a blanket, a glass of water, a pillow for her back. Nancy planned to spend the night in the guest room and drive back up to Boston in the morning.

"This is the best way forward," Nancy said to Grace in the hallway, before they headed to bed.

"It is." Grace held both of Nancy's hands in hers. Tears welled in her eyes. "Thank you, Nancy. Thank you for driving down. You're such a good friend. I don't know how I would have gotten through tonight without you."

"Well, I almost blew it!"

"Yeah, you almost did." Grace sniffed. "But it was the push I needed."

"I've been meaning to ask you...maybe now is not the best time..."

"No, go ahead. What? You've been meaning to ask me what?" Grace tilted her head.

"Did you ever try to find the baby you had to give up in college?" Grace looked down toward the floor. "Oh, I'm sorry," Nancy said quickly. "I didn't mean to upset you! Forget I said it."

"No, it's okay. I did try. I wrote a letter to the maternity home a few weeks ago, but haven't heard back. Even though it's painful, I think about her often—about the woman she's becoming, where she might live, what she might look like. Whether she likes books."

"Oh, honey. I'm sure she's gorgeous and smart, with a heart of gold, just like you." Grace cried softly. "Come here." Nancy held her tight. "You had no choice back then, Grace. You did the right thing. Just like you're doing the right thing now, okay? Now try and get some sleep."

"Thank you, Nancy. I will. Good night."

"Sleep tight, sweetie." Nancy kissed her cheek and went off to bed.

A few minutes later, Ed and Grace stood at their his-and-hers sinks brushing their teeth. "Should we look into getting a nanny?" Ed asked, smearing toothpaste onto his brush. "I remember Lois and Robert had one they were very happy with. That was years ago, but maybe she's still available."

"That's not my biggest worry at the moment," Grace replied. "I've been thinking, what if the college doesn't grant me tenure when they find out that I'm pregnant?" Grace looked at Ed in the mirror. "I'm supposed to meet with the board in mid-August, just before the fall semester starts up again. By then, I might not be able to hide it."

"Well, I think you could try," Ed said. "You've worked hard for this, Grace. I want to support you in any way I can. Maybe once they grant you tenure, once that's set in stone, you can take a semester off or something." Ed rinsed his mouth with water and spat into the sink.

"I recently heard about a professor over at Franklin and Marshall College who wasn't granted tenure once they found out she was pregnant," Grace opined. "Less than half of female professors in Pennsylvania are on a tenure track to begin with. And of that small percentage I've heard countless stories of women being pushed out of their jobs for any little reason at all. I can't let that happen, Ed. Of course, I'm over the moon about this baby, but I don't want to sacrifice my career, everything I've worked so hard for. Just think about how much time and money I spent getting my education!" The more Grace talked about it, the more frustrated she became.

"Try to calm down, Grace," Ed said, hugging her. "I'm sure it will all work out. We'll make a plan. We can always ask for some legal advice. I know at least two lawyers through the country club. Just go to the meeting as planned, get them to sign off on your tenure, and we'll go from there." Ed switched off the bathroom light and they went toward their separate bedrooms. "Goodnight, Grace. I love you." Ed gave her a warm smile, lingering at his door.

"Goodnight, Ed." Grace went to her bedroom and drew down the sheets. She lay down and switched off her bedside lamp, but something didn't feel right. She looked up at the ceiling, turned onto her left side, then her right, then switched her light back on. She sat up, swung her legs over the bedside, slipped on her slippers and went to Ed's room. There he was, lying prone in the dark. "Grace?"

"I think I'll sleep in here tonight, if that's okay," Grace said as she crawled into bed behind him and put her hand on his shoulder.

"Of course that's okay."

"Goodnight, Ed."

"Goodnight, Grace." Ed squeezed her hand, kissed it, then laid it back on his shoulder.

Grace felt Ed's breathing and listened to the comforting sound of his breath. She imagined what their future together as a family would be like. A warm feeling traveled through her, as she pictured Ed playing catch in the backyard, fishing out his old baseball mitt from the attic, or sitting down in a too-small chair at a too-small table and sipping out of a miniature teacup. She saw them each holding a little hand, swinging their child up into the air on a count of three as they walked to the nearby pond to feed the ducks. All at once she was flooded with a deep gratitude for the man beside her. A man who wanted nothing more than for her to be happy, and who had always respected her. Grace kissed the back of his neck, and fell into a deep sleep.

The next morning, after hearing a thousand times how ecstatic Ed was about the baby and the endless list of things he thought they should take care of before it arrived, the doorbell rang. Grace turned to Nancy and excused herself from the breakfast table. She opened the front door to find a delivery man standing there with flowers.

"Grace Gilmartin?"

"Yes, that's me."

He handed over a large bouquet of fragrant blooms, with a small note attached, and returned to his truck. The card read:

I'm so sorry. Can we still be friends? - Lois

Grace smiled. She tucked the note in her pocket and brought the flowers inside.

Ed had already left for work, clicking his heels together like Fred Astaire on his way out the door, being silly. Grace had made him promise not to tell anyone until after their next doctor's check-up. But seeing his excitement, she doubted this request would be honored. After slurping down the last sip of her coffee, Nancy set off for Boston. She had a long drive ahead of her and wanted to get home before dark.

It was Saturday, July 16, one week to the day since the Member Guest dinner. In an effort to normalize things, and with the confidence instilled in her by Lois's note girding her, Grace decided to go to the country club. Now that she was committed to the narrative of having her husband's baby she felt better, more settled. It was as if she'd finally spotted the lighthouse on the shore after weeks alone on a dark stormy sea. Thoughts of Peter still haunted her every day, but seeing Ed so happy and finally telling him she was pregnant had brought Grace a much-needed sense of peace and calm. Ed's excitement was infectious. This was her second chance to be a mother and she didn't want to screw it up. She didn't want to lose *this* baby. *She* knew who the father was, and that was all that mattered.

♥♥♥

As Grace walked into the country club she kept her head down at first, avoiding eye contact. When she reached her usual chair, Lois was the only one sitting on Queens' Row. Jane was swimming laps, and there was no sign of Barbara or Ethel, which was a bit of a relief. Olga was still being detained by the FBI and, it was safe to say, would never be coming back to the club again. Grace still could not believe that Olga had wormed her way into their group and that something so globally consequential had transpired in their sleepy little town.

Lois looked up from her book. "Grace, I was hoping you'd come out to the pool today." She stood up, walked over to Grace, and gave her a hug.

"I'm a horrible person," she said as she leaned against Grace's frame. "I don't know what got into me, letting Ethel convince me to run that stupid story. I guess…I guess I was jealous."

"Jealous? That's ridiculous! Jealous of what?"

"Well, of you and Barbara. It just seemed like you two were becoming so close."

"Close? We're no closer than the two of you are."

"I know. I know. I was being foolish," Lois said. "Ethel had me convinced that something nefarious was going on, and that, combined with my jealousy, and our flagging subscriptions…I mean, come on…you, of all people, having a tryst with a Secret

Service agent? I'm ashamed. And I'm so, so sorry. Grace, can you forgive me?" Lois squeezed Grace's hand and looked straight into her eyes, awaiting her friend's verdict.

"I was hurt, Lois. I really thought we were better friends than that. But yes, of course. I forgive you."

"I was acting like a schoolgirl, and I won't ever let that happen again," Lois said soberly, as she continued to squeeze Grace's hand. "I have one question, if you'll allow it. Is it true?"

"Is what true?" Grace pulled her hand back.

"Are you pregnant? I have to admit I've been wondering for a while now."

"Yes, it's true, you little sneak. It's still early, so only Ed knows for now. Well, Ed, my doctor, and now you."

"Congratulations! I'm so happy for you. You and Ed must be absolutely over the moon!"

Jane had climbed out of the pool and was wringing out her hair as she walked toward Queens' Row.

"Can we tell Jane?" Lois whispered to Grace.

"Tell me what? What's going on over here, ladies?" Jane asked, one eyebrow arched.

"Go ahead and tell her, Grace." Lois puffed out her chest like a proud hen as she nodded toward Jane.

"Okay, but please promise you'll keep this between us...Jane, I'm pregnant."

"Wow! Grace, that's amazing news!

"Shhh, keep it down! And please stop leaping about." Grace laughed, looking left and right to make sure no one had heard. "As I was telling Lois, it's still early, so that's the main reason I haven't told you ladies. But I'm also trying to keep it under wraps, because I'm up for tenure and this could ruin everything."

"I get it, Grace. Our lips are sealed." Jane gave Grace a long hug while a puddle of water pooled beneath them on the pavement.

The three of them sat, soaking up the sun's rays. Mary waved at Grace from her chair, "Thank you for my final grade, Professor Gilmartin!"

"It was well deserved, Mary!" Grace called back.

Grace lay surrounded by sunbathers on their stomachs in their *chaise longues*, wrists dangling and bracelets clinking. She took a deep breath and thought about how much had happened in just two months' time. She thought about Peter, about the twinkle in his eye and his dimpled smile that always seemed to say everything was going to be alright. She looked up at the brilliant white cumulus clouds floating overhead and could have sworn that one of them was shaped like a heart.

11
Tenure

5 weeks later: August 24, 1960

A symphony of cicadas reverberated off the handsome brick buildings of Gettysburg College. The grass was crispy and brown, having taken a beating during the hot, dry summer. Students wouldn't be arriving on campus for another week. Grace, now visibly pregnant and full of nerves, walked to the English Department in Glatfelter Hall. She was to appear before the campuswide Tenure and Promotion Committee, which consisted of the head of the English Department, the dean, the provost, and the president of the college itself, to hear whether or not she would be granted tenure. Ever since Grace was a teenager, she had dreamt of this day—when she would find a way to parlay her love for books and words into a viable career.

Academic tenure was the acme of what college professors strove for. It meant more security—guaranteeing their job until they chose to retire—more money, and more status. Grace had spent the better part of a year assembling her portfolio, which included teaching evaluations, a list of committees on which she had served, copies of her publications, and recommendations from outside scholars.

Grace stood outside Glatfelter Hall, looking up at the hulking building for a moment. She took a deep breath, wiped her sweaty palms against her dress, and swung open the door. Her kitten heels clicked loudly as she lugged her leather briefcase up the stairs to the second floor. She reached into her pocket and squeezed the handkerchief that Peter had given her the night they were reunited at the White House. Since his death, she'd developed a habit of carrying it with her, especially when she was facing a challenge, which was pretty much all the time these days

Grace could hear voices as she rounded the corner. She knocked lightly on the door and entered to find the four old men who controlled the college—and her fate—sitting in a row behind an imposing table, arms folded. Kings' Row. A beam of sunlight streamed through the large stained glass windows behind them, highlighting their bald but revered heads, as they made hushed comments to each other.

The dean cleared his throat. "Professor Gilmartin, welcome! You're right on time. Please, have a seat." He pointed to the lone chair across from them.

"Good morning, gentlemen. Thank you," Grace said, smiling. She could feel their eyes on her protruding stomach as she sat down. She removed her portfolio from her briefcase and placed it on the table in front of them.

"May I?" The head of the English Department reached over and opened the portfolio, spreading its contents out in front of the other men. After a flurry of pointing and nods of approval, the committee members drilled her with questions for a full hour. First they wanted to know all about the articles she had written and her future research plans. They then turned their attention to her teaching evaluations—all of which were reviews from Grace's students about her relatability, engaging style, and clear passion for literature. Grace felt herself loosening up after the first five minutes. She embodied the message: "This is what I love to do, I'm good at it, and I deserve to be here."

"Well, what does your husband think about all

this, his wife being granted tenure?" The dean asked. Grace felt her hackles raising but quickly shifted gears.

"He's not happy about the prospect of more microwave meals, but he's very supportive." They all laughed.

The head of the English Department looked over his glasses at Grace. "Why do you enjoy being a professor, and why do you think you deserve tenure?"

She paused to gather her thoughts. "I've dreamt about being a professor ever since I was a little girl. You see, I never really had a mentor myself, so it's gratifying to be able to give my students the support and encouragement they need to thrive." The head of the English Department nodded.

"Grace, if you'll excuse us for a moment?" The president of the college stood up and walked toward the door and the other men followed.

Grace tapped her foot as she waited for them to return with their decision. *There is nothing I would have done differently*, she thought to herself. She felt a strange quiver in her stomach and realized that it was the baby kicking, for the first time. That tiny flutter reminded her that she was not alone, not anymore. She had been given a second shot at motherhood—that word still gave her pause—and she knew how rare second chances were. It was high time she let go of the shame and guilt she had felt since that fateful semester "in Quebec." But it had started before that, hadn't it? It had started the day her mother walked out the door. The sense of abandonment she'd felt at thirteen had never really left her. She had filled her mother's shoes when she'd left, stepping into a role that should never have been demanded of her in the first place. Her mother's decision to leave had robbed her of her childhood and left a gaping hole in her psyche, but if Grace was honest with herself, she understood why her mother had left—and she forgave her. It was time to let go—of the mother who haunted her past, of the mystery baby she had abandoned herself, of the lover she had lost twice over.

Grace looked around the empty room and steeled herself against rejection. No matter what happened, she would get through it. It finally hit her that she was strong and always had been strong. Though she was terrified, she was standing proud here today asking for a new shot at life, at experiencing childhood through her baby's eyes, at love.

After what felt like an eternity, the men filed back in and stood across the table from Grace. She got to her feet to receive their final decree.

"Professor Grace Gilmartin," the head of the English Department said, acting as spokesman, "after careful review of your portfolio, we are all in firm agreement that you should be granted tenure here at our esteemed institution. Congratulations!" He smiled widely and reached out to shake Grace's hand.

Grace gasped, "Thank you, gentlemen!" She felt like she was floating on a cloud. It was like the time she'd first set foot on the Smith campus, like the moment she'd first met Peter, like the day she graduated from Columbia with honors. She felt giddy, elated.

The department head glanced down at her stomach. "When is your due date?"

"The beginning of February," Grace said, her smile deflating. Her face blazed and her heart rate shot up. Had she just ruined everything by saying this? Could they revoke her tenure?

"You may consider taking the second half of the spring semester off to spend some quality time with your baby," the department head said. "We can hire a temporary replacement for you, until you start back in the fall. Either way, your position is secure."

"That's wonderful! Absolutely wonderful!" Grace said as she shook each of their hands to seal the deal.

Grace decided to check her college mailbox before

going home to tell Ed the good news. On her way she saw Trudy, busily typing away at her desk.

"Professor Gilmartin! How did it go?"

"I got tenure!" Grace beamed.

Trudy stopped typing and rushed out from behind her desk to hug Grace. "Well, congratulations, dear!" Grace could feel her stomach pressing up against Trudy. "You deserve it. Not just the tenure...." She looked at Grace's burgeoning bump and smiled.

Grace's face flushed. "Thank you, Trudy. I haven't seen you all summer. A lot has happened." Grace ran her hands over her stomach. "I'm just going to check my mailbox quickly."

"Sure."

Grace's mailbox contained a single white envelope, from St. Mary's Maternity Home. Her mouth became dry and she felt a stab of excitement.

"Oh, yes, that came for you yesterday," said Trudy. "Strange place to get mail from, don't you think?"

"Yes. Yes, it is." She placed the letter in her bag. "I'm going to go home now and celebrate with Ed."

"You do that, sweetheart. I'll see you next week—I still can't believe freshman orientation is this week-end!" Trudy sat down, adjusted her glasses, and resumed typing.

"I know! Time really does fly." Grace glanced at the precious watch Peter had given her all those years ago. It was already 12:30 p.m. She knew Ed was waitingat home for her, dying to know the outcome of her meeting. Grace wasn't ready to open the letter yet. She wanted to bask in the glory of this wonderful news. She walked the two blocks home in a sort of daze, riding the high and replaying the words that had been exchanged in the meeting in her head. When she got to the house, she found Ed assembling a crib in the nursery—formerly the guest room—upstairs.

He wiped sweat from his forehead and smiled when he saw Grace. "And…?"

"I got tenure!"

Ed ran to her, picked her up gently, and swung her around. "Grace! Congratulations!" He placed her back on her feet and kissed her. "I didn't want to say anything until it was certain, but I booked us a place on the shore this weekend to celebrate, a cottage in Cape May." He rested his hands on her shoulders. "I figured, it's your last weekend before classes start up again. It will be like our second honeymoon."

Grace was touched by this and hugged him tight. "Oh, Ed. How very thoughtful of you. What a great idea. The shore!"

As they held each other, a soft breeze made its way through the nursery window. The silence felt comfortable as they embraced. It was in that moment that Grace realized the secrets she carried were more like precious stones than ugly birthmarks. It was okay to hold onto them, and to let go of the shame. She used to wonder, *How can someone strive for perfection, when they're already flawed?* But now she knew that something one of her favorite writers, John Ruskin, had said had been right all along—that imperfection is essential to all that we know in life. She would never be perfect, and that was okay. More than okay. She was living, she was loving, she was following her dreams. She was Grace Gilmartin. Grateful Grace.

Acknowledgements

I honestly didn't think I had another story in me after finishing *Place* in 2021. Writing is *hard*! It might be the hardest thing out there, after performing open-heart surgery. But inspiration comes from the oddest places. In my case, inspiration came from a framed menu I inherited from my Grandma Betty, who passed away in 2015. It's a keepsake from the night she attended a dinner at the White House in 1960, during Dwight Eisenhower's final term as president. I thought, "there has to be a story there!"

That menu, combined with the first-person stories my grandmother, who was a wonderful storyteller, told me about the time she'd spent hobnobbing with the who's-who of Gettysburg at the country club, while her own children (my father and aunt) played with Eisenhower's grandchildren, got my creative juices going again. Having grown up in Gettysburg, I had always wondered what it must have been like to have a prominent couple like Mamie and Ike dropped into the social mix of such a small town.

Once I had seized upon the White House dinner as a jumping off point, I knew the Eisenhowers would be the axis around which I could spin a drama, against the powerful backdrop of my historic hometown. The final piece of the puzzle was the idea to incorporate the Eisenhower Era iteration of Queens' Row—the permanent fixture of women occupying a row of chairs at the country club, where I had also spent summers as a child. Slowly but surely a story took shape, and it had the added benefit of enabling me to learn more about Gettysburg, a place that holds a special place in my heart, along the way. That's the beauty of historical fiction.

I want to extend my gratitude to my mother, Valerie, who bravely faced a situation in high school similar to what Grace endured. By sharing her story, she allowed me to understand the psychology of weighing such a momentous, life-changing decision alone.

I could not have written and produced this book without the help of a long list of incredible people. Thank you to the members of my online Monday morning "Write or Do Nothing" writing group—Janelle Hanchett, Henri Colens, Mickelle Weber, Julia Bailey, and Hayley Rose—who provided the inspiration and push I needed to set words to paper. And to Andie Huber—no relation—for helping me get the "bones" down for this novel, and for being my accountability partner. I also owe a debt of gratitude to Lauren Valbert and her mother, Jane, who shared their experiences at Smith College, to Els de Koning of the Breukelen Bridge Club, who explained the complex rules of bridge, and to my parents, who gamely answered all of my random questions, from "What did they sell at G.C. Murphy in the '60s?" to "How do you keep score in golf?"

Thank you, too, to my beta readers—Henri Colens, Hayley Rose, and Ross Patton—for applying a fresh set of eyes to my manuscript, and to Lisa Doctor for her valuable editorial feedback and guidance. Adding nuance is the hardest part of the revision process and, by asking the right questions and providing the necessary prompts, Lisa helped me make my characters come alive.

Thank you to my dear childhood friend, Leslie Trew Magraw, who edited the book in its final stages, and provided the cherry on top: the introduction. We've always shared a love for Gettysburg and I'm grateful we had the opportunity to work together to produce a piece of work that takes place in our hometown.

There's a lot that goes into publishing a book, beyond getting the words right. Thank you, Joe Webb, for your beautiful cover art. When I picture Grace, I picture the woman on the cover of this book, with her gold watch. I had a mock-up of the book cover done early, tacked it next to my desk and used that as my inspiration each day to write. If the cover's there, and the title, the book *has* to happen, right? And to my team members at Amsterdam Academy Press—Glenn Doherty and Cigdem Guven for their work on the book cover design, Rebecca Blunden for her developmental editing and proofreading skills, Lisa Hall for her layout magic, and Koos van Leeuwen at Tipoprint—thank you for helping me create the book of my dreams.

From the very outset, it was the support and interest of my friends and family—especially that of my husband, Joost, and our children, Noor, Mary, and Tom—that gave me the confidence to keep going. If you believed my daughter Mary, you would think I was a *New York Times* bestselling author. Most importantly, thank you to my readers. There are a lot of books out there, so thank you for giving your time and attention to mine.

Printed in the USA
CPSIA information can be obtained
at www.ICGtesting.com
CBHW061524100924
14345CB00031B/350

9 789090 374595